10- T
don

Calendar Boy

Calendar Boy

Andy Quan

NEW STAR BOOKS
VANCOUVER
2001

New Star Books Ltd.
107 - 3477 Commercial Street
Vancouver, BC
v5n 4e8
info@NewStarBooks.com
www.NewStarBooks.com

Quotation from "Better Off Without a Wife" by Tom Waits, © Six Palms Music Corporation (ASCAP). Reproduced by permission.

Cover by Rayola Graphic Design
Cover illustration by Sam Shoichet
Typeset by New Star Books
Printed & bound in Canada by Transcontinental Printing
1 2 3 4 5 05 04 03 02 01

Publication of this work is made possible by grants from the Canada Council, the British Columbia Arts Council, and the Department of Canadian Heritage Book Publishing Industry Development Program.

CANADIAN CATALOGUING IN PUBLICATION DATA

Quan, Andy.
Calendar boy

ISBN 0-921586-82-5

I. Title.
PS8583.U3318C34 2001 C813'.6 C2001-910328-X
PR9199.4.Q36C34 2001

Contents

Acknowledgments

To me, writing is about community. It is about not only how I and others move in the world, but it is about the support and advice that I've received from family, friends and strangers for my creativity and my writing.

The stories in this collection have been inspired by many people, and have been through countless edits in response to helpful advice from editors, friends, colleagues and mentors. If you've ever read one of these stories before it's appeared in print, you've played a part in them. Thanks to all of you for your help. Editors, both those who accepted and who rejected these stories, have also helped shape my prose into more finished forms. *Calendar Boy* owes particular thanks to fine editing and eagle-eyed proofing from Rolf Maurer, Viola Funk, and Sophie Ambrose.

I also acknowledge New Star Books for doing this with me, Arsenal Pulp Press for encouraging gay writing in Canada, Penguin Australia for agreeing to bring *Calendar Boy* to Oz, and the Asian-Canadian Writer's Workshop for supporting my manuscripts.

I send my love to friends from Pearson, Trent, CWY, Trois-Pistoles, York, IPC-Denmark, Expo '92, Belgium, London, Sydney, Toronto and Vancouver – with a special nod to Dean Perry, Marcelo Vela, Derek Hall, Kim Anderson and Thomas Kevin Dolan.

"How to Cook Chinese Rice" first appeared in *Queeries: An Anthology of Gay Male Prose* (Arsenal Pulp Press, Vancouver, 1993). It subsequently appeared in the magazine *Geist* and the *Asian-American Writer's Journal*. An excerpt from "Hair", entitled "Bald", appeared in *Queer View Mirror* (Arsenal Pulp Press, Vancouver, 1995). A shortened version of "Immigrant Song" appeared in *Contra/Diction*

(Arsenal Pulp Press, Vancouver, 1998). "Hair" was published in *Circa 2000: Gay Fiction at the Millennium* (Alyson Publications, Los Angeles/New York, 2000). "Calendar Boy" and "What I Really Hate" appeared in *Take Out: Queer Writing from Asian Pacific America* (Asian American Writers Workshop and Temple University Press, 2001).

Andy Quan's website is at *www.andyquan.com*.

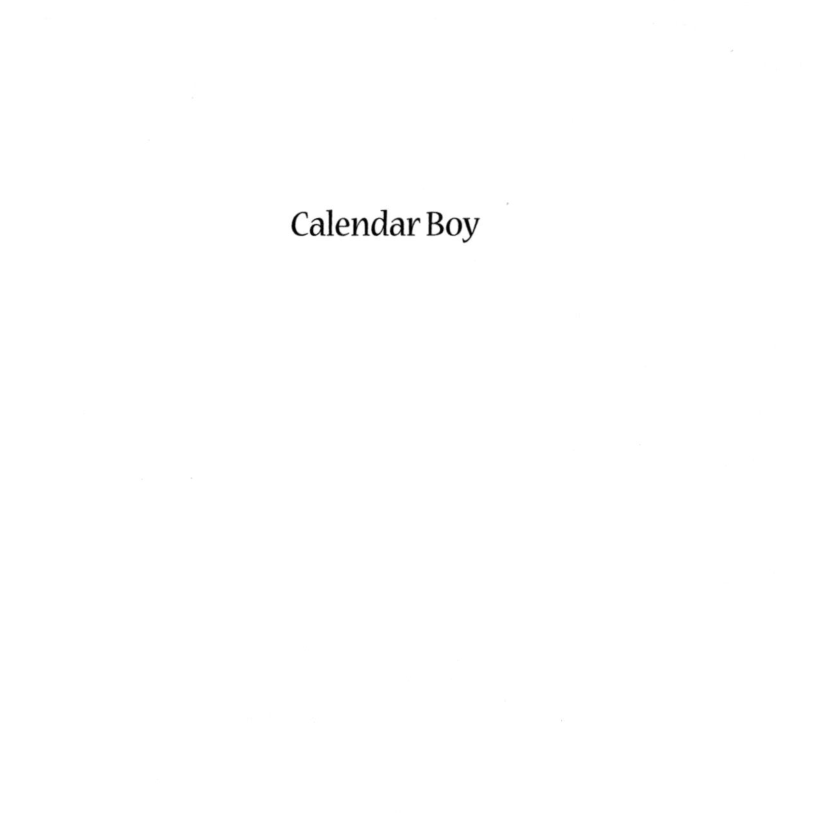

Calendar Boy

How to Cook Chinese Rice

It's not necessary to have a rice cooker or a wok to cook perfect delicious white rice every time. Here's how:

1. Selection

If you want your rice to turn out like it does in Chinese restaurants, you have to use Chinese rice. This is the long grain stuff; the short fat sticky rice is Japanese. Don't buy Uncle Ben's processed rice, or rice with the faces of white people on the boxes.

The genesis: I came seven years after my first brother and five years after my second, Dragon following Tiger and then, the Cock. Uranus was on the horizon when I was born, the planet of reversal; also, my House of Love was out of alignment with the other planets. Armstrong landed on the Moon. The general stress of the sixties ending caused disturbance in the womb. My hypothalamus was larger than my penis; a renegade gene cruised down the family tree from the grand-uncle who moved to New York and was never heard from again. I was born partially clothed, a red silk cloth wrapped around mid-section, patterns of bamboo and cranes stitched in. I arrived with a full head of hair.

2. Measurement

How many people are you going to serve? Rice tastes best fresh but you can always use it for fried rice if there is any left over, and rice reheats well in a microwave. Regardless, use half of a Chinese rice bowl (or about half a cup) per person.

I'm listening very quietly as if someone is going to say, "Get out, you don't belong with us." There are only six or seven of us in the room. A girl is talking about life on the streets of Vancouver.

She says: I remember one time, three of us girls out at the amusement park with Rickie, our pimp, and the ferris wheel rising up in the sky and the sunlight making diamonds out of its metal frame. Us, wrapped in sticky fur coats, looking out at other girls, laughing with their friends. Wishing to be them more than anything else anywhere.

Also: no one on the streets wants to sleep with a black

man. It's bad but it's true. Girls are scared. But you know the best? The Oriental men. They're always polite, very clean, and you know? They come quickly. That's the kind of customer you want.

3. Put the rice in a pot

Now, put the rice in a pot that has a tight-fitting lid.

Man in disco. Empty. A weeknight. Shirt too small. My hand wrapped around sweaty beer. I lean against a rail next to the dance floor. His white flesh approaching. Glowing fluorescent. Layer of exposed skin above belt like fat steamed chicken. Eye glint. Bearded grin. "Hey. Me and my friend think you're kind of cute. Maybe you could join us."

No. Flashing lights. I'm waiting. Speakers shake like a vacuum cleaner switched on. For a friend. Like a house being cleaned. Like all the dust in the room swirling into one place. No. Visible only with sunlight pouring through the window. Maybe later. Feel guilty you're not helping. Mother's reproachful eyes. Man walks away.

Later he follows. Heavy disco beat. Brushes up against me. "Hey. I had a Vietnamese boyfriend." Bodies sweating, bodies thrashing. Asks again. No. Fat man, his eyes like an outstretched hand. No. Shake my head once. Quick like a flick of a chopstick. Like cocking a gun.

4. The important part

Now, rinse the rice in cold water until all of the starch comes off and the water is relatively clear. If you don't do this then your rice will be starchy. It will stick together in soggy clumps. This is how white people usually cook their rice.

When I was ten, I naturally gravitated to the other Chinese boys in our class, two in particular, Ronald and James. We talked about computers, hockey cards, mystery books. Not about girls like the cool boys, not about sweaty secret mysteries like the clique of Greek boys with their names of ancient philosophers and emperors.

I drifted apart from them at fourteen, about the same time that Christine Greenstern came up to me with the revelation that all Chinese people were smart, had eyeglasses and were good at math. This must be something genetic. True, we all worked as library monitors, entered the big math contest, and two of us were still taking piano lessons. All of us had good marks. I supposed that it was time to go searching.

At eighteen, I climbed the stairs to my first meeting of the university's gay group. I peered around a corner and peeked into a dark room: thin trails of smoke twisting upwards like genies escaping without granting any wishes. About a dozen men sat on three rundown sofas, all of them blond or seemingly blond. A stray limp wrist flung here and there. Few of them say hello.

5. Cover it up

Cover the rice with just about an inch of water, 2.5 centimetres or up to the first joint of a normal-sized index finger.

I'm thirteen. I've hidden my ruler in my bedroom drawer. No one is home and the curtains are drawn.

How long is it supposed to be? Where do you measure it from? Will it grow when I do?

Six years later, Philippe Rushton, professor at the University of Western Ontario, concludes that as an Asian, I have a relatively small penis.

Two years later, I am kissing with my lover Ian on his living room sofa. His other lover, Brian, comes in through the basement, rambles up the stairs, sits down.

"I'm so stoned. Whoa." He moans, getting up to leave. "Carry on. I'll just go into the bedroom."

He stops in the middle of the room, and invites us in.

"You have a long cock," he remarks, the three of us on the king-size bed.

I look at him. "Really? I always thought the opposite."

He reaches over. "Yeah, really."

6. Confidence

Have confidence. Cooking, like all other meaningful activities, requires a state of mind where you believe in yourself. Repeat after me: "I can cook rice."

I'm twenty-one and still haven't learned much of anything. But it's the summer of the Gay Games in Vancouver and my heart is bursting like popcorn, with the sight of same-sex couples sightseeing, hand-in-hand, as natural as starfish on tidal rocks, as the mountains against the bright harbour.

I've volunteered to help at the bodybuilding competition. Giddy with anticipation, I eventually get assigned to the steamy weight room in the back of the theatre: short, wide women and men oiling their bodies and pumping weights. There's nothing to do because too many volunteers were assigned for too little work. I'm free to do what I please.

I roam the hallways greeting people as if at a party, eyes wide and energetic. I tell myself that I never had the opportunity to be a goofy hormone-pumped adolescent. I hid my sexuality in asexuality. Hey, I tell myself, this is my chance, and I even have my camera!

Later in the day, I pass by a room where a couple is packing up to take a lunch break after the morning's pre-judging. I talk to the woman first, that's safer. Then the man, piercing blue eyes and short perfectly spiked platinum blond hair.

"Hey, where are you from?"

He smiles at me. My knees buckle. "San Francisco."

"Wow, you guys from California are hot." I wipe imaginary sweat from my brow.

Jeremy is an accountant but spends all the rest of his time training for competitions. He points out the difference to me between those on steroids and those who are not. Suddenly, I notice that while his body is perfectly shaped, it's not as big as many of the others. He won't even come close to winning in his weight category, but maybe with Rita they'll have a chance in the pairs competition. He has an open, naturally friendly west coast manner, tells me I've got four years to train for the next Gay Games.

"Hey, can I get a photo with you?"

We give the camera to his partner.

I look at him again. "Without the shirt."

He rolls his eyes, I make excusing noises, but he obliges. I get my photo: funny Chinese kid with a smug smile, arm around the shoulders of a tanned mass of taut muscles. I shake his hand and bound off, completely pleased with myself.

Kane was another man, intense of manner with flashy workout clothes, prematurely whitish-grey hair, and blue-grey eyes. He didn't look like the other bodybuilders at all. He wasn't all that much bigger than me, though the diet of the last months and no water for a day added appropriate bulges and lines. I find out that he's only been training for two years; it was his personal goal to compete in the lightweight category.

We walk to the weight room together and sit chatting. I notice Jeremy across the room, slouched in a chair, legs up on a stool. I try to catch his eye but he seems angry about something.

By the end of the day, I've given my phone number to

Kane, who later turns out to be both boring and self-centred.

That summer night, I'm walking across the Granville Street bridge, the concrete span hovering over the blue-black water, the stars out like the first practice of a new choir. It hits me then, and I picture Jeremy's face, annoyed, reflecting off mirrors and iron bars.

I think that anyone else would have known. But I didn't. While I was flirting with him, so obviously that it wasn't obvious to me, he was flirting with me, a skinny Chinese kid who never imagined that someone who looked like all his fantasies could ever be interested in him.

Have you ever been in a fortune cookie factory? The flour mixture falls in small circles, gets cooked on both sides, a tiny paper is placed inside by a flurry of hands. Then, before it cools, it's folded over in one direction, and the ends are brought down in another, gracefully like a crane taking off in flight, the neck crooking down, the wings rising up, drops of water from its legs spreading in concentric circles on the lake. This was my summer, my city, the Gay Games: the rare sights of graceful, beautiful, strange birds soaring into blueness. And also sweetness, the city on one giant pancake being heated up, changing substance, forming into something different from what it was.

I cracked open my cookie. I keep my fortune with that photo I took backstage at the bodybuilding competition. The fortune says: HEY KID, NEVER, EVER, SELL YOURSELF SHORT.

7. Heat it up

Cook at high heat until the water begins to boil. Then turn the heat down to medium-high; the water will still be bubbling away at a good rate. Wait until the water has boiled down to the same level as the rice.

The most visible and well-known gay man in my small university town was an older man, an actor, who dressed in drag and sang a song about lemon trees. His weekly column appeared in our university newspaper as "Gay Voices," a flowery ongoing series of memoirs about a childhood in an eccentric British household in southern Ontario. All the illustrations for the column were either viny art nouveau or old newspaper graphics of men in top hats and women in flapper dresses. All the posters and advertisements for the university's gay and lesbian dances featured stills from either black and white Garbo films or lesbian vampire thrillers.

When I complain about this introduction to gay life a few years later, I'm scolded by a master's student named Barry: "That was camp and camp is not ethnocentric! It's our forgotten history. It was poor black and Latino drag queens and bull dykes out there on the front lines at Stonewall, hauling away at riot police and kicking over fire hydrants!"

I try to imagine myself at Stonewall, shouts flying over the top of me from lips like scythes, salt and anger and resistance flying into open wounds.

I try to imagine myself in black-and-white, languishing in tones of grey, perhaps in a housecoat, maybe in silk pyjamas.

I have no reply.

8. Steam it up

Then, put the lid on the pot and turn the heat down to absolute minimum so the hot steam can cook the rice.

Underwear parties are sweeping Toronto's underground: the latest, greatest, hottest thing to do. By the time I go to my first, the trend is dying. What else is new? Before I go, I tie my long black hair back into a tight ponytail. I try to look masculine and clean-cut.

We shed our winter gear at the door, try to fit our clothes into flimsy plastic bags. The doormen put our bags in a room full of such bags, mark numbers on our hands.

Arrows from the check-in direct us out the back door and through the parking lot to another building. We run against the cold, fly through the door, up the stairs, pay some guy a big cover charge and enter: a room full of dancing men in Calvin Klein athletic shorts, not even the boxers. Gay men are so cutting edge.

We've just come from the university dance, the Homo Hop, and that's how we look, a bunch of university kids, half a dozen of us, no one confident enough to go barechested, and why would we? All these gym bodies trotting around: stacked together, the collective hours at the gym could build railways, erect monuments, great, tall phallic ones like in the mythic cities of Europe.

Scout the place: big to me, but one of the guys says it's nothing, only one floor; one he went to had three levels, all crowded, with different music on each one, even a whirlpool on one floor. This one has a darkroom in the far corner – the lightest one I've ever seen, streetlight moonglow revving though the windows like a brand new Harley-Davidson. Few men are doing anything. Lots are coming around, walking through, waiting, watching. I follow suit, like one in a V-shaped flock of birds heading to the warmest place possible.

The leaders move by instinct and watch no one else for clues. They fall into various types and are somehow the same: these ones greyish hair, thick and brawny; these ones short brown hair, smooth and tightly muscled; the others light-haired and tall and doll-like. They are with each other, the rest of us all on lower levels of the hierarchy.

The light from the window makes all of us overexposed. Muscular back, on his knees, goes in on leather jacket, bare chest. And I don't think they are beautiful because I'm not thinking, only seeing, and knowing somewhere they are only images, warmth in my groin, MTV, Madonna's dancers, porn advertisements at the back of the newspaper.

Later, I see another Oriental man, short and slight like a bird. Groups have now formed in the room; two men kissing and a train of two or three men behind each of them pushing in close, reaching, moaning, others in the corners against the walls. The Oriental man moves around these groups gracefully like a shadow, like a breeze, and disappears down into the clusters of tall men with their high cheekbones and square jaws and pinkish-white flesh. He re-emerges, shifts place, disappears again into another group. On the other side of the room, I stand in the crowd, silent and stupid, watching him bob up and down in the waves, but never float on top, the other men's jaws and lips locked on each other's mouths or chests, and him down below, negotiating the undertow. People enter and leave, the crowd ebbs and flows.

I walk around this party. I do not stoop. I look people in the eye. No one returns my glance.

9. The waiting game

Steam for about ten to fifteen minutes. Hopefully, you'll be able to tell when it's cooked.

My parents chase a good Chinese restaurant until it closes or the cooks leave. They follow leads to find the next one: Honourable Grasshopper, a family of Charlie Chans.

Father orders a bowl of house soup from the back of the kitchen. It's communist soup, he explains, for anyone who wants it, it is always on the stove to be shared. I go through a whole childhood eating this soup, a clear broth with huge pieces of carrots swimming around, a piece of fatty beef. It becomes my motif to eat a bowl before the meal, and one after. The sun rises, it sets, then it is called a day.

We eat here with all of my parents' friends from the city, our relatives, visitors from out of town. If it is a special occasion, the owner puts a tablecloth over the shiny brown formica. The room smells of honey and garlic.

That restaurant closes. The next one as well. And another. And again. New ones open. Father orders dishes in Cantonese; they arrive, sizzling in earthenware pots. A clatter of plates, steam rising to the ceiling.

I am afraid I will never get another taste of my special soup and I will never again receive something I know exists but cannot describe.

10. Don't peek

Resist the temptation to open the lid before the cooking process is done. All the steam will escape.

The subway leaves me on Yonge Street, only a block away from Church. My steps lift me higher and higher like the tall apartment buildings lining the sidewalks.

I spend the day here, moving from restaurant to café, grocery store to boutique. I read the gay newspaper: comic strips first, then the front page, skip to the events section, scan the personals. My eyes wander to the beefy models in the ads for gay phone lines. I look up, see a man in tight jeans walking a bike spray-painted yellow. I wonder about his secret lives. My eyes follow his footsteps all the way up

Church Street to that distant point on the horizon where all the lines of telephone poles, pavement, buildings, and wires intersect.

Then I cross the street. I move so quickly that I'm sure no one can ever catch up. I am afraid that I'll never find my way in anything but action. I am required to move like this. If I halt for even one faltering second, the whirring of a thousand maple keys pulling downwards and the roar of a million angry bees will tear me apart.

11. Ready?

Serve it any way you want. Thank my mother for the recipe.

Higher Learning

When I look back at my younger self, my naïve self, I am embarrassed at my utter lack of savvy, that sixth sense that could have pointed me to where I wanted to go. Anyone could have told me that the gay life I was seeking would not be found in Peterborough, Ontario. *Montreal, Toronto, New York*. Big Urban Centres. They were the places to go. Instead, because I'd heard about a progressive university with a "highly visible" lesbian and gay population, I'd flown to Toronto, hopped onto a bus, and arrived an hour and a half later. Besides, I was a tree-hugger, a neo-hippy, an eco-kid: other categories that were supposed to make up the student population. I'd read the environmentalist tome *Small is Beautiful* and thought "of course it is."

Now it was time to turn ideals into reality. But the day I

arrived to start my first year of university, all the stores were closed and there was not a bus in sight. 'Where am I?' I thought.

"It's Sunday," explained the bored blank-eyed teenager at the Donut Hut, the only sign of life for miles.

Sixty thousand didn't sound like that small a population but it felt that way. Peterborough was a tidy conservative village, far from the coast that I grew up on and far from my big city comforts. Still, I had escaped from my parents' home and I felt gloriously anonymous. No matter how small or isolated a place Peterborough was, I was determined that here I would learn what it was like to be gay, what it meant to fall in love with another man.

~

The posters for the first gay and lesbian dance of the year were taped to lampposts and bulletin boards, ripped down, and sometimes new ones put up to replace them, depending on the enthusiasm and energy of the volunteers.

A dance like this was rarely held in semi-rural Ontario. It was awaited not only by students but also by a handful of faculty, men from the town, and even men from the outskirts of Peterborough. Up the stairs to the small cafeteria of one of the colleges: lights were dimmed, tables and chairs cleared off to the sides of the room, a sound system set up on one end of the cafeteria, a bar at the other.

Wandering awkwardly through a crowd of perhaps fifty men and a few women, I ran out of places to walk to. The music was nothing to write home about either, not that I would write home about something like this – it would be another few months before I would write *that* letter to my parents. I had a few brief chats but didn't hit it off with anyone. Maybe I expected too much. So I danced, hoping to swirl myself into a state of ease, to some obscure disco song at not a loud enough volume.

The first time I went to a gay bar was with an artsy crowd of straight friends. They liked it because it was "cool," the drinks were cheap, the atmosphere daring. To greet, they kissed each other on both cheeks and looked absolutely ecstatic and bored at the same time. After a while, I started going to those bars by myself.

Still, it would take a long while to feel at ease, to understand the choreography. I'd arrive and look around at a roomful of older men and didn't know why I would try to talk with them. Why I should. Why I didn't. What would I have said? Besides, how could I talk with the music so loud?

I could have said they had hungry eyes. I'd once read a tawdry newspaper exposé about a dimly lit gay bar filled with lonely men with hungry eyes. And it might have been true. But the truth was that I was oblivious to the whole of it. Music, flashing lights, a dance floor. I thought people went there to dance. Eventually, when I did catch on to the main purpose of the bars, it was only the most obvious and desperate men that stood out to me. The rest had practised, learned blank expressions and to my eyes, mostly came with friends.

That's why I learned to dance by myself and I enjoyed it most when the floor was empty. I would reel and swing around like ocean waves, try to fit my body into the music. Now I'm more self-conscious, but back then at my first university dance, I could block myself off completely from the world like a snail in its shell while the dance floor started to fill around me.

Tim left at the same time as me, around one or two in the morning. He had drunken watery eyes and a slight sway.

"Hey," he said, "can I walk you home?" He was an upper-year archaeology student of medium height and slight build. I'd seen his articles in the university newspaper's *Gay Banter* column. He signed his name to them. I wished I could do that too.

"No, actually. I live just around the corner."

He staggered along as he walked and I was embarrassed. At the time, I considered public drunkenness a sign of vulnerability that I neither cared to show nor witness.

I was too naïve to know what he wanted.

"Come on," he pleaded, "just to the door."

"No, really, I've got a roommate and I don't want to wake him up." I wondered what he would do, with or without a roommate. Did he want to kiss me? I'd never kissed a man before; I'd never kissed anyone, in fact, on the lips – the important kind of kissing. But I didn't want to kiss him.

"Just to the door," he repeated.

"No," I replied. "Good night." I watched him stumble off towards the centre of town and I went to my room.

Do you know how some people seemed to know about sex all along: the language, the rhythm, the possibilities and dangers? Not only the act, but the prelude and the afterwards, the words that you don't hear and how to talk with your eyes and body.

It took me years to even begin to learn.

I slept fitfully and did not remember my dreams in the morning. When I awoke, I thanked my roommate.

"For what?" he asked.

"Oh, I don't know," I replied. "It's just nice to come home to someone."

~

It was a confusing courtship. Somewhere in the recesses of my mind, I knew that I was attracted to him. But on the surface, he was a friend and though I had a reputation for being a bit intense with friends, I expected nothing more.

Peter's dormitory room gave me no clues, not that I was looking for any. He had a postcard on his bulletin board of a busty woman in a pink bikini. The books on his shelf were similar to mine but a few years more advanced. He studied politics too.

I'd drop by between classes, before meals, sometimes in the evening. I thought nothing of it. Students always dropped by on each other, no need for appointments. I was in a new place. When I met people I thought would be friends, I pursued them with gusto. I had no experience with relationships so I tried to make do with passionate friendships.

Thus, finding out that the friendship I was chasing was turning into a relationship was confusing. Almost as bewildering as the first kiss on the day that he admitted to me that he was gay and he could tell by my attention that I wanted more from him than I'd said.

We stood and faced each other. My head was whirling. He leaned into me. I closed my eyes. They always close their eyes in the movies and I couldn't imagine keeping them open to look at someone so closely. But I'd never kissed anyone before. Ever.

Peter, who had a wide jaw and an ample mouth, opened wide and with his tongue making slow circles, he closed in on my closed lips. The top of his mouth upon my nose, the bottom near my chin, I felt as if swallowed alive. I thought of whales, a large octopus, and cartoon fish with puckered lips. He grinned sheepishly and taught me to open my mouth.

I was pleased to have my first boyfriend but I still didn't

quite understand what was going on. Why was he calling every day? I had old friends from high school that I'd known for longer, liked better, but certainly didn't talk with as regularly.

We broke up regularly during the first weeks. He would say that he couldn't go through with it. It was too early. Too fast. He wasn't ready. He wasn't really gay. People would find out. All of this, I took in my stride since it had arrived so easily and unexpectedly, it didn't surprise me that it would be taken away in the same way. He would ask advice from a girlfriend who I quickly grew to dislike.

"Bridget said I shouldn't be so scared." Peter at the door of my room. "Bridget said that no one suspects a thing." As a gay acquaintance walked by and winked. "Bridget said it's strange you don't call me as much as I call you."

Oddly, my recollection is not of talking even though talk was one of the things I was best at. I think I must have kept inside my head like a genie in a bottle, poor Peter on the outside trying to rub his way in.

It didn't work. I didn't know I was supposed to be in love. I had far too much of the world to explore to spend all of my time with one person, especially when I needed time to myself as well. It was the year I came out to my parents and the season that my grandmother died and a friend committed suicide.

And Peter? What I didn't know about him was that his dad was an alcoholic, that he'd blocked out whole sections of his childhood, that he was used to fighting in relationships rather than peace, and that he needed me to be far more than I could ever be.

Also that I wasn't his first boyfriend, though I don't know why I thought I was. He had had an affair with an older man in his small town all through his teenage years, and then had several confusing teenage courtships with girls while he tried to fit in and be as normal as everyone else.

He came to me crying after a few months. "It hurts so much."

I didn't know how hard it was for him or how strange my response must have seemed. "I don't want to cause you so much pain, Peter. This relationship isn't doing you any good."

A completely logical, rational response. We broke up and never spoke again, another thing which confused me since I still hadn't worked out the difference between a relationship and a friendship.

I will, however, always remember him for it was with him I had my first sexual experience. It started innocently enough, a little kissing in a music practise room, a piano and a bench, a metronome, a locked door. It was supposed to be soundproof. With practise, I had learned to fit my mouth to his and thoroughly enjoyed it.

After a time, he put his hand on my crotch, hard through my jeans. He looked into my eyes, a serious expression that I couldn't interpret. "Are you scared?"

"No." What did I have to be scared of? From what I had

read, you didn't have sex until you really knew the person, and besides, first base was necking but second base was petting.

Peter didn't know those rules or if he did, he wasn't paying attention. He unbuttoned my pants, pulled down my underwear. I was erect. I looked at my penis as if it belonged to someone else. He was on his knees and moved his mouth towards it.

How could I not have enjoyed the warm sensation that rushed through me? But I also remember looking at him and the walls around me, random sheet music pinned up, a notice for university events. My body became more and more excited until it let loose its tension. My eyes remained the same, looking away, looking down at him.

He looked up at me, brushed back his hair with his hand. "Do I look a mess?"

I walked around in a daze the whole next day and wondered if I was still a virgin.

~

At the end of that first year of university, Darren came into my life. It started in the midst of exams and since I was leaving soon after, I didn't think anything was possible between me and this handsome guy I was flirting with who had come out just a few weeks ago.

It began quietly. I had started signing my name to articles in the campus newspaper's *Gay Banter* column. Soon after,

I found a note in my mailbox from Trish, a sharp-witted vegetarian sociology student who I sometimes shared meals with in the cafeteria.

"You speak for many of us," she wrote in careful, rounded letters. "And I wish I could be brave enough to do what you did." I'd teased her about her diet, not because I disapproved, but because I liked meat too much to do without. For this reason, she'd signed her note with a large cartoon carrot.

Afterwards, we would meet for tea in her bedroom. When the pot was empty, she would take the tea bag out and throw it against the wall above the heater. "The trick is to make it stick!" Laughing on those quiet nights, a tea-stained wall beside us, we lay back, small confidences rising like clouds above us, words darting in and out like swallows, finding words to describe our attractions, how I loved men and how she loved women.

In time, Darren would knock quietly, enter the room and sit in on our conversations, never saying anything.

"What do you think, Darren?" I asked once. "You just seem to sit there like a fly on the wall."

"Just call me fly on the wall."

~

I started visiting him after that. One time I asked, "If you're attracted to women, why not define yourself as bisexual? I don't see a problem with that."

"I don't know," he sighed. "But for now, I'm gay. I'm definitely gay."

We only slept together once before the end of the year, and that was all we did: sleep together. He had come up to my room earlier in the evening, beer on his breath, hugged me and said he was going, he knew I had an exam the next morning. Then he paused and turned around.

"Would you spend the night with me?" he asked, softly.

"Well, OK," I replied, equally softly. "But spending the night is all I can promise, nothing more."

"I'm not asking for more."

I grabbed my backpack and we headed out the door.

The night was warm and intimate and I can still recall the shade of morning light as I got up to leave the room for my exam. My arms were sore from holding him. I don't know how he managed to sleep. I was glad we'd spent the night as we had though. After the messy first relationship with Peter that winter, I didn't want to have sex.

Well, that's not entirely true. I did, in fact, want to have sex but I wasn't sure that I could feel in control of the situation. I certainly didn't feel that way with Peter, who seemed to know exactly what he wanted, and in fact probably did, since I wasn't his first lover. That block between the head and the heart, mind and the gut. Something always felt wrong. I wanted to talk about it but didn't know what to say.

I've learned that one can communicate with not even a whisper. But at that time, first with Peter and then with

Darren, I thought I had to talk about it first. Posters, television, advertisements – all told me to talk first, then do it. I was becoming sexually active in the age of AIDS, before the talk shifted from "high-risk categories" to "high-risk behaviour." I was scared. I was one of the chosen.

Later that summer, I visited Darren at his home on Lake Erie. I had only been out that way when I was a child but it all came back to me as the bus rolled along, fields of grapes tying together a flat rolling landscape.

The afternoon I arrived, we had lunch and went walking down at the beach, so different in this part of the country than my own. A whole city lay across the water and the sand from the water's edge up to the first cottages was filled with a million tiny shells with ready-made holes so that you could string them together if you wanted to.

The water amazed me too. Out on the lake in an aluminum rowboat, he jumped into the water and I followed in my jeans, t-shirt, and the bus ticket which I would later find in my pocket, which we would laugh over and try to dry out. Everything was so clean, felt so clean, I couldn't believe it. Ocean water leaves its traces on you the moment you leave it and when in it, the smell of salt and seaweed and detritus assaults your senses. This fresh-water lake was so different, strangely sterile, but so soft, I thought, as I grabbed onto Darren who clung to the side of the boat. Could anyone see us? I scanned the shoreline. I felt that I had so many things to say. In the end, just one: I want you, will you hold me tonight?

I spent the whole day wondering how to say this. We took a final stroll on the beach. Night fell. I had resigned myself to a night alone as his parents were upstairs, but he shut off the main light, climbed into bed with me, and turned off the bedside lamp. I got my wish, and he held me. He pushed for more than that and now, I wish I had let him go further.

~

He never replied to the letters I sent over the summer but when I got back to university the next year, I learned what he'd been up to. Alana had long flowing red hair, dark brown eyes that danced in the light, and an open and easy manner. She tried to make me feel as comfortable as possible and I suppose I felt more important for Darren having told her about me. Their summer whirlwind romance led to them moving in together that fall. When I saw them walking hand in hand on the town's quiet tree-lined roads, I knew it would never be so easy for me. They have a child now who I imagine is beautiful.

~

I hear they have satellites that can read a license plate in Times Square or a newspaper on the streets of Moscow. I figure that if they can do that, we should cultivate an expression of knowing something that they don't, since they can certainly see our faces as well. Can they see us, too, as we leave parties and slip into the night, as we stumble along this grid of right angles and streetlamp shine? Can they see the look of wonder and question in the eyes of a child locked out of his house or separated from his parents on a day at the beach? Could they see me those days wandering in my university town pondering dances, first boyfriends, and jealousy?

Once I had a vivid nightmare about sand: dry waves passing over my body like the shapes visible at low tide left by ocean waves. Only these were set in motion. Each chink in an impenetrable wall shone one beam of light and at the same time made one grain of sand fall upon me. It was everywhere, locked into the curve of my eyelashes, pressed under my fingernails and toenails, in my saliva and my skin. I rose up to scream but the weight and density of the sand absorbed everything. No movement nor sound broke the stillness. I'd found freedom and it was suffocating me.

Often during that first year of university, I thought, I miss the ocean, I miss the mountains, what am I doing here? Soon enough I'd be going, the year would finish. A few cycles of that and I'd be out of university into a larger world.

My biggest fear at the time was that leaving, I'd find everywhere else to be exactly the same. Years later, I was proved half-right and half-wrong: things do stay the same, but sometimes, love comes in waves and it seems that the whole beach has shifted oh-so-slightly and for the better.

At the time though, I'd try to make myself believe that love and happiness would all be possible. But every once in a while, I had doubts. The sand hit my skin, grain by grain. I wouldn't know until I left that when I stood up, the sand would fall like a spell. Some grains would stick and some would not.

Meeting Henri

Work is slow so Kim and I are chatting at the bottom of the conveyor belt. We consider running over to the bakery down the street to buy a cinnamon bun to split and decide to hold off until later.

When we actually work, we're restockers: taking things from the back of the store and putting them out where customers can find them. Like memory and the human brain, we carry things from recesses, corners and storage shelves and put them out to be accessible. I realise this is a silly way of romanticising my job, but it keeps me going.

Margy jogs up and we ask her how dance classes are going. She's only working part-time now, and doing two, three, even four classes a day. Kim dances too and they sometimes attend the same classes. I'm not sure what we were talking about before Margy arrived, but it must have been men.

Once, when I was younger, coming out was enough to create intimacy with friends. Suddenly these people were chosen to share the biggest worry in my life. I gave them my trust and need. They were honoured by my confidence, surprised by the novelty, and happy to keep a secret.

As time passed and being gay became easier and simpler, I needed to find a similar topic: personal, inexhaustible, a key to new friendships. So, I came to talk of men with new friends, straight women friends at least, and other gay men: compulsively, obsessively, endlessly. Finally, I was allowed to be the giggly high schooler that I never was and affirm my sexuality to boot.

I know I'm in trouble by the way that Margy says his name. "You should meet this guy in our dance glass. He is soooo gorgeous. Today, we were sitting in a group and he put his head up against my knee and I . . ." she stops and giggles, lets out a cry of lust. "I got to stroke his hair! His name is Henri," she tells me. "*And* he's gay," she continues looking at me. She laughs again, "You know who I'm talking about, eh, Kim?"

Kim nods and explains to me: "Yeah, he's very handsome. He's from Québec and has this real energy. Everyone thinks so, men and women both."

"Is he attached?" I ask.

Margy shakes her head, "Do you know, Kim?"

"No, I've never asked."

"Well, I guess we'll have to find out," I say trying to be convincing. "And you guys are going to have to start introducing me to your handsome gay dancer friends."

~

In a nightclub. He's with a few friends. I overhear his name and know that it's him. He is as handsome as they said, tall and dark.

I approach him discreetly. "Hi. Do you take dance classes with Kim and Margy?"

"Yeah," he replies, surprised and moves over so I can sit down.

"How do you say your name properly?"

"It's Henri." His voice is charming with a sparkle of energy.

"Hen–ri," I repeat. "Pleased to meet you, my name is Douglas . . ."

~

A few key words, and I'm hooked: Handsome. Attractive. Gay. Phew, my fantasy world kicks in immediately. Is he available? What does he look like? How old is he? What colour hair? Is he a nice guy? I say jokingly, "Do you think I'm his type?" Even though I don't know what type I mean. Asian. Canadian. Twenty-one. Not quite wise in the ways of the world.

Margy laughed when I asked her the last question but she told me about the rest. Henri has light hair, he's about her age – twenty-six –, she doesn't know whether he's available. He's not too tall, about my height, five foot seven, and just about everyone likes him. She told me that one of their dance instructors last summer decided to call him Horny just to give him a hard time.

"Probably because he had a crush on him," she laughs.

"He's a terrific dancer too," says Kim who's just joined us. "Graceful and strong. I could just watch him for the whole day long, he dances with such expression!"

"Well, how do you know he's gay?" I query.

"Oh, I just know," replies Margy, and Kim nods in affirmation. "Everyone knows. With the amount of women chasing him, we would know if he wasn't gay."

"I'd love to meet this guy before I leave for university. Margy, you giggle when you say his name, and Kim, your eyes light up. I should see what turns you women on."

Kim laughs. "Oh, he just wants to *see* him, that's all."

I think about that and decide she's right.

~

Henri comes into the store, and the women employees look his way, raise their eyebrows. I'm working, putting out some shirts on a rack. I didn't know that he was coming to the store; Margy in the back of the store is giggling with this knowledge.

"Do you need any assistance?" I ask and can't help noticing his great body, light hair, obvious energy.

He asks a question and speaks with a slight accent.

"Oh, are you Margy's friend, Henri?"

He nods as if he expected to be asked this.

"I've got a coffee break now. Do you want to walk over to the bakery?" I look at him hopefully. At the bakery, we make plans to go out to dinner.

~

You wouldn't think that gay men would be hard to find in Vancouver's West End or at the city's dance clubs and bars. I'd stare out into a sea of dancing bodies on a Thursday night thinking 'where do all these men come from?' and 'where do they disappear to in real life?'

I'll ask this for years. Bars are supposed to be for meeting people, or so they say. And I never knew exactly why I couldn't. Was it my age and innocence, eyes wide like those of a deer in front of headlights? The colour of my skin? The energy that I gave off? Years later an American friend, a PhD student of Eastern philosophy, will exclaim, "Vancouver men? They NEVER talk to you in bars." A light will go on in my head. I'll nod in agreement.

Growing up, my senses would come alive at the sound of the words "gay" and "homosexual." I was desperate to find others, observe others, to know others. But who? The men who paraded on TV and films were swishy, sparkly, outrageous. Why were these men part of my family? Extravagant aunts who tried to outdress everyone else at the party. And why couldn't I see my image in any of them?

Lesbians and bisexuals would remain invisible for a few years yet, but I did start my investigations to find other men like me. I found a meeting for gay youth at the Vancouver Gay and Lesbian Centre. It was friendly enough, a small group of guys since it was summer. Apparently, during the school year, the numbers got bigger.

"Oh, I never would have guessed about you," said one of the guys, Lance.

'Me?' I thought. Picked last for sports teams. Never had a girlfriend.

"Your voice is so deep. And there's nothing *ob*vious," he put an emphasis on the first syllable. "God, the more nervous I get, like when I'm in a room full of hostile straight boys, the camper I get, my voice gets out of control and high." He smiled sheepishly. "I'm less camp when I'm around people I'm comfortable with."

"I'm surprised. I thought it would be the other way around." Is my voice deep? Do we all want to sound straight, whatever that is?

Sometimes, I find heterosexual men deeply attractive. Not all of them, and certainly, the ignorant I can do without: those who can't recognise oppression at all and think feminism is a dirty word. But the ones I fall for live in a world of attractive innocence, a world they trust in and so are shocked at rather than used to some of the goings-on.

A cute straight boy with that open look of concern. It makes me weak.

I didn't go back to the group. There was no one there that I wanted to pursue for romance or sex and, at the same time, I didn't feel enough kinship to go just for the company. Or maybe there was too much kinship – in all of our own ways we were outcasts and whatever that had done to us, we were marked by it. Being around gay men, whether friends or lovers, was going to take some getting used to.

~

"Why were you interested in meeting me?" he asks grinning. He's confident, assured yet sparkles with an innocent radiance. Margy talked with him, found out that he would consider a date and then set us up together.

"Well, what did Margy say?" I say coyly.

He pauses. "She said that she had a friend that she thought I might get along with and would I be interested in meeting him."

"Oh. Well, that was well done. I've got a good story to tell." I proceed to recount how Margy and Kim talk about him and how could I not be interested in someone who was described in such glowing colours? "They don't seem to be wrong so far," I add.

Henri laughs, not uncomfortably. We look into each other's eyes.

~

I joke with Margy, tell her that I should give her a note to give to Henri with my phone number and a provocative message.

"Yeah, right," she giggles and I laugh too.

"But can I send you on a mission," I plead, a little more serious. "Find out if he's single. Or interested in a blind date."

"OK," she agrees. "Tomorrow at dance class."

She bounds off to continue working. I grab my crate of Nalgene water bottles and head off to the camping section. I wonder what I'd say if I were in her position: "Are you seeing anyone now?" "Are you single?" "I've got this friend and I told him about you . . ." None of these queries seem to work well in my mind.

I don't know how some people find it so easy, the language of love. How they know the borders between innocence and knowledge, between heavy desire and lightweight flirting. I like to fantasise that everyone is just as confused as I am, but I'm not so sure.

I think I consider myself lucky that I was never consciously in love with boys my own age. Boys as thin as me with pimples and foul mouths. Even the teen idols at the time didn't do it for me. Feathered haircuts on big-eyed angels. Girls would tape the photos to their lockers: Shaun Cassidy, Scott Baio. Instead, I seem to recall a swimsuit model buried deep in a thick Eaton's catalogue that I found in our basement. Tarzan fascinated me too in a thinly disguised way. Mike Henry, a hirsute ex-football player, was the one I liked best.

However, I had no idea what I would do with these objects of lust. I think the fantasy went as far as them showing up at my bedroom door and looking me in the eyes. Sex, I knew, was something both embarrassing (because of the way adults refused to talk about it) and hilarious (because of the way it made kids giggle). But what was it like, really? And when would I get it?

~

It starts with a caress. When he takes his hand away from my skin, I wonder if I'm trembling. I decide I'm not. I'm just very excited. Henri lies down on his stomach. Window light falls across his back and highlights a landscape of muscles.

It's early evening. His apartment is dark for the most part but the natural light tumbles inward across floor and furniture, fabric and skin. It's my favourite light, I decide, by which to see another person, delineating the ripples and creases of the body, colouring the complexion an exquisite daylight white. My heart beats like a child's footsteps running to retrieve a lost object. And his breath upon my skin like feathers, until stopped by the clashing of tongues, we fall into each other, we become twenty-fingered and four-legged, a tangle of hair and appendages.

Hours later, I tell him that it was the best sex I've ever had. He continues to massage my back, and I see his face in the corner of my eye. He smiles and leans over, brushes his lips against the side of my neck.

~

When I next see Margy at work, I can tell immediately that she hasn't talked to him. She greets me but her body signals that she has no more to say and because of that, we keep a distance. Besides, it's busy and there is work to do.

Later she steels herself and explains. "I'm sorry, I didn't talk to him. I hardly saw him the other day and he left as soon as the class ended. Besides," she says, drawing closer. "To tell the truth, I don't feel all that comfortable asking. Maybe at a better time, out for coffee or something, but not out of the blue." She shrugs, looks apologetic but relieved for being honest.

"That's OK, Margy." I shrug and smile. "I understand." And for all my daydreaming, I do.

~

A year later, I am back again in Vancouver on summer break from university. I'm going out to meet Margy and Kim at a local bar after their dance class. Margy has cut down on her classes and Kim has stepped up on hers. They often have a drink afterwards with the other dancers.

When I arrive, I hug each of them and look around. I can't tell if everyone is together or if the seats in the bar are just too close together. But introductions are soon being made to a mixed group of men and women.

"And this," points out Margy with a hint of a smile, "is the famous Henri."

A small, lithe blond man shakes my hand and flashes a grin. "Pleased to meet you," he says as I join them.

I remember then the last news that I heard of him. Margy did find out at the end of last summer that Henri was in a relationship, a long-term one, "practically married," she said. They had been together six years and were happily in love.

Henri tells me this during our first long awaited conversation and mentions his partner's name, Christopher, with obvious affection. Henri is as handsome and beautiful as I expected. And quite real. He excuses himself and turns to answer a question, joins in talking with his friends, people he knows and is used to. He becomes engrossed and I turn my chair slightly to face their circle.

I watch for a moment his fine features in the act of conversation. I admire the sight and turn away. For Margy has let out a familiar giggle while talking to another dancer. And he has raised his eyebrows towards me in a way I am quite sure I understand.

What I Really Hate

Chinese people, if you study Chinese history, are very hard to handle. In normal times, they are obedient. They respect senior people, they respect authority. Chinese people are flexible. They can suffer to an extreme that most of the European race cannot imagine. So elastic. But on the other hand, just like a spring, if they get beyond the limit, the Chinese race loses all reason.

– CHAO YAO-TUNG
RETIRED CABINET MINISTER
TAIWAN GOVERNMENT

Sometimes they get it wrong. By "they", I mean the laughing gods, the chief scientists, the potion-mixers and spell-casters. By "wrong", I mean that by clumsy stirring, the tiniest ill measurement, a drop of sour milk, the experiment is ruined. By "the experiment", I mean, well, *everything*, really.

Like, why can't Chinese drink alcohol without turning red? Or, why do old ugly white men chase young Asians in gay bars? Or even, why do I have this name, Buster?

I mean, there's no short form, no nicer nickname, and my middle name is much worse and a well-kept secret. I managed to find out that Mother had enrolled in a night school literature course at some point in my pre-history. She never actually finished the course, but I got Tennyson as my middle name.

Buster, however, was incomprehensible, and I could uncover no explanation. "Huh, so demanding, so ungrateful," when I would ask my mother. Father on the other hand would simply smile, blankly, at a practical joke that I was not willing to identify as me. He made it seem like it was Mother's doing.

I'm not sure whether I see my name as an inheritance, but I do see it as a cultural trait. Who else would have such a name but a child of Chinese immigrants? A Fontaine, Lester, Leonard or Dexter. I feel marked by it, and am essentially too conservative (arguably another inheritance) to consider adopting something different. Although I do know of a Chinese acquaintance who dropped his original name (also top secret) and renamed himself Tony, after the lead character in *Saturday Night Fever*. As well, a husband and wife who both changed their names to something luckier after consulting with a Chinese numerologist.

What I think I really would have liked to have as a cultural heritage is something else. A toughness, a lack of sentimentality. The Chinese are a brutal people. This is something I can admire. For example, none of the fondness towards animals that pervades a pet-crazed west. Dog soup, why not? Better yet, stir-fried. Who cares about endangered species? The Chinese will cut the bollocks off any animal unlucky enough to have rubbed the ancient soothsayers the right *or the wrong* way.

It's not just animals that we're talking about here. Only a generation or two ago, families would give away children to other relatives, if there were too many mouths to feed, or if one family was short of a son. No hullabaloo, it was just done. Imagine the tabloid story that would make today. You could sell that to the *Star*.

Another tale: a girl is dying of multiple sclerosis. Her father's family *can* afford the new and unproved treatment, but only if they sink a considerable portion of the family savings into it. They weigh the risks: certain financial hardship for the family but the girl may live; certain financial hardship for the family but the girl may die. Pragmatism ruled; you know the end of the story.

Now, I'm not saying that I'd like to be able to turn my back on the dead and dying, but I would like some of that practicality and lack of sentimentality, that kind of working with the world rather than fighting it. Thicker skin, really: stand-in-the-rain, water-rolls-off-me kind of thicker skin. But instead, the words go right into me, the incidents pour inside. My internal organs have little room to do what they are supposed to do.

So, what is blocking up my breathing, interrupting my heartbeat, pressing on my liver? A partial list: every time someone comes up and asks me where I'm from (where I'm *really* from) before they've asked my name; every time someone tells me I look like I'm eighteen even though the hair's going and the baby fat on my face is long gone; finding out that the person talking to you has a special interest in Asian culture; the ones who insist on approaching and talking to you when you've not made eye contact, smiled, or shown any friendliness whatsoever; the ones who treat you like you're too stupid or unassertive to order your own drinks or get your jacket from the coat check – they try to do it for you.

What's worse is the ones that come up and think they're so clever. *Oh yeah? Born in Canada. You're not Chinese! You're a banana! White on the inside, yellow on the outside.*

OK, I suppose I should be sympathetic. I can relate to this, you've been given concepts and it's a pleasure to finally be able to match them up. Like when you first see a Tasmanian devil in the zoo, and you get to compare it to the one in the cartoon. Or how about when someone describes what baked Alaska is, and when you actually get to see it. The problem is, if you think that the wallaby with rabies is the Tasmanian devil and the oddly shaped pavlova is a baked Alaska. In truth, no sympathy for wrong guesses.

When it comes down to it, I think they should stand there and scratch their heads, and say, "go figure." Rather than, *oh, you're Chinese, you're gay, you're born in Canada*: guessing what that means. In fact, I'm checkerboard. Through and through, two-tone abstract art, multi-coloured swirl painting. Plaid, baby, I'm plaid, so out of fashion I'm in fashion and so stylish I'm on my way out. I don't go with anything you own.

Anyway, what I really hate are gay Asian clubs. They're the worst. I mean, what a bad joke: a race of people who can't handle alcohol. Sweet elixir: gin and tonic, frothy beer, the bite and softness of good red wine, bubbles up your nose champagne. I wouldn't want to see us as a race of Londoners, drinking at the pubs after work until we fall down at closing time at eleven at night. Or drunken Scandiwegian-Germanic tourists crawling through Spanish and Portuguese cobblestone streets, sangria and sherry spilt down the front of their shirts. But at least, we should be able to toss back a few brewskies. A roomful of soda waters with lemon does not ooze sex appeal.

Why do we have a separate club night anyways? Does this put us into the category of leather night, rubbermen, underwear parties? Are we a fetish or are we a theme party? Here you can see my arms in front of you, stretched out, a movie star, a pop star, a poster child, a peace campaigner. I'm saying, "Why can't we all get along?"

But I'm being facetious. I know why there are separate nights. It's because we're supposed to share a culture, and have the opportunity to be in the majority, to celebrate what we have in common, and be together. And also because we don't fit in at regular gay bars, that we need a relief from them. If you don't know why, it's probably not worth explaining.

Or maybe what the point really is here is sex. Isn't that what it always boils down to? The fact that we can't get sex at other clubs, and don't know whether some white-black-latino-whoever is going to just look right through us, or that guy we're interested in is going to turn his back, but before doing so, snarl, as if to say, how dare you? How dare you even think about it? Since we're not sexual, not masculine, since they don't go for Asians.

So, really, what we're talking about is, *yum, yum, how am I going to get some?*

Now, listen, I have tried to enjoy myself at these clubs. I've got my Asian complex of *duty*. In fact, I'd stayed away from the first gay Asian nights I'd heard about. It was a gut reaction – when I think of Asian men, I think of my weird cousins or my uncle who shakes my hand when he sees me only as a way to grip it and swing me around to look at the back of my head. "You need a haircut, nephew." Square black-framed accountant's glasses, his thinning hair slicked back.

So what makes me change my mind is the time I'm in this mainly white club (they're all mainly white), striding along and see three Asian boys sitting off to my left, all kind of girly, dressed in the same flashy way. I walk straight on by since what have I got in common with them? Am I supposed to do some hey-Asian-brother hand signal each time? That's when one turns to the others, scowls and says "*Gao.*" Now, I hardly speak any Chinese, mostly food words like other Western-born Asian kids. But I did struggle through a few years of Chinese school where they taught us useful phrases like *"The cow ascends the mountain. The moon is bright."* And we also learned the animals in the Chinese horoscope (very useful), one of which is the dog. *Gao.*

So, I'm a dog, am I? Angry for a moment, but it made me think. Maybe I should get to know Asian gay guys. Not that I'd want to go out of my way, but maybe I'd been actually avoiding them more than if they were just a neutral generic Mr. Wonder Bread White.

So, that's when I ended up at the Long Yang Party. First Sunday of the month. I get there and the guys at the front desk are ultra-friendly. Have you been here before? Do you want to get on the mailing list? I get this feeling like I'm in Communist China, and we're all supposed to be this big happy family with Little Red Books tucked in our back pockets. Some Chinese people I meet, it's like they adopt you, *hallelujah* (except most are heathens), we can do tai chi in the park together and sing Chinese opera.

Up the stairs to check out the crowd, it's mostly Asian, the music is regular dance club beat-beat-beat, the bar-boys are white and have their shirts off. I'm scared before we even start because I've heard the rumours. Gay Asians suddenly hauling out a karaoke machine, the dancing stops, it's a KARAOKE party. Or at this club, I know it's coming. At midnight, inexplicably, they cut the dance tracks, and start up the cha-cha music. And what's worse, everyone knows the dance. Cha-cha-cha. No wonder they think Asians are geeks.

I look around for something I relate to, but it's no good. In the people, the place, the air itself. What is this idea about a big happy Asian family, like A for Asia is like a big teepee tent construct, and we're all underneath it? Granted, I've met a lot of *camp* Asian boys but I look around at the crowd, and I ask: What am I supposed to share with these people? Malaysia, Indonesia, Thailand, Singapore, China, Japan, Korea, Vietnam. Hello? Different countries. I mean, Thai guys, for example. I don't get them. They giggle all the time, are always happy, always trying to be nice. No wonder white guys who are into power and domination and talking about themselves all the time like to have boyfriends like them. Wallflowers.

Or OK, let's narrow it down to just the Chinese. My grandparents were villagers in a feudal countryside. Is this anything like growing up wearing Mao blue in Red China? Or born into an overpopulated noisy cauldron like Shanghai or Taipei or Beijing, which by the way is still Peking to me. The language, even if I did speak it, isn't even the same, and even if it was, would a rich city boy from Hong Kong put down his mobile phone to talk to a country hick like me?

The song playing is not one I can dance to, and I know no one here. Time for a drink at the bar. None of this Campari, white wine spritzer stuff. I ask for a scotch on the rocks, try to make eye contact with the bar-boy when he gives me my change (keep it, I might have said) but he barely glances up.

Scanning the room once more: I can recognise others who are Western-born. How we walk, how we move, the clothes, the people we're with. I can't explain it. But there are hardly any of us. What I see is dozens of twinkies, chicken, young boys from abroad, clothes and speech at too high a volume, the bulge of a mobile phone barely hidden at the waist. Demure, giggly, and oblivious.

After all, the ones who weren't born here were raised in a society where they were the *majority* not the *minority*. They haven't been snubbed all their life; they don't expect racism so they don't see it. They're here for a good time, papa's paying for a Western education. They don't even know they're being oppressed.

And what's the big idea chasing after the old ugly white guys in the bars? That makes the oldsters feel invincible; the rest of us have to fend them off. I don't understand it at all. The theories are: respect for elders, veneration for ancestors, no youth-oriented culture, no bias against the aged.

But listen, at a certain age, you can't get it up. Are we going to take it as a given that adage about trading youth and beauty for age and experience? More like they're trading it for a ticket to the west, a place to live, fine dining, free rides. Which I can relate to, I'd like a boyfriend with a car too. But what's worse than going into a bar and seeing all these pairs of cute young teenage Asian boys with Yoda from *Star Wars*, Santa Claus, Bob Hope? What's a self-respecting Canadian-born Chinese guy supposed to do?

A short brightly dressed Asian guy jostles by, dragging his Italian-looking boyfriend by the hand. Cute. I catch his eye. And I hate that. Hate cruising other guy's boyfriends. Can't stand it. If he looks at me, I think, *creep!* If he doesn't, I think, *aren't I good looking enough?* This one looks. The next one doesn't.

I've figured it out though. Why I do it. It's because in other clubs, I don't know if guys are looking right through me because they think I'm ugly, or because they wouldn't consider touching an Asian with a bargepole. And if someone comes up to me, I don't know if it's because of me, or because I'm Asian. Or if it's somewhere in between, what's the ratio?

So when I see a white boy with an Asian guy? The heart jumps and the other sensory organs come to life, a beast waking up from hibernation. Whether I'm right or wrong in the end is irrelevant, but for now, what I smell is a gay man who *must* in some way be attracted to Asians. Spit forms inside my mouth, my chest and shoulders draw out bigger, and I can't stop myself, I'm helplessly without control. I cruise them, maybe even before I have a good look.

The Asian half of the pair looks over with a look of death, squints his eyes to say *he's mine*, and prances off.

I grab a handful of potato chips from a table in the corner and stuff my face. Who cares if I'm seen looking like a slob, my mouth full of food? They advertise free snacks. What have we got? Dim sum? Prawn crackers? Canapés? No. Chips and pretzels, a bowl of peanuts, and if I'm not mistaken – no, I'm not – there's a few plates of homemade biscuits. How classy, it's like a lesbian bake-off. Asians are so cheap.

And the boorish rice queens? That night, I didn't meet any and other nights I did. I won't go on at length. What to say about a group of people who say they were Asian in past lives, have never mastered the art of subtle cruising, and in conversations, consistently cut off their Asian boyfriends in mid-speech? And furthermore collect art and boys in equal numbers, and display them the same way: glass cases, photos, receipts, authenticity certificates, or plain old boasting. I mean, I go for certain physical types too, but it's a variety. Isn't only being attracted to Asians kind of like eating only pasta for breakfast, lunch and dinner? Or rice, more like it.

Enough of that. But I will tell you, after that first Asian night, I went back. Not every time, but on and off over the years: *Red Lantern, Rainbow Room, Phoenix, Dragon, Katana*. Even though I didn't enjoy myself, I couldn't keep away, each time hoping that somewhere in that room would be the person who was looking for me: a guy who happened to be Asian, and an Asian who happened to be me.

So that's really why I hate gay Asian clubs: the gold-diggers, the rice queens, the tackiness and forced togetherness. The cha-cha-cha, the chicken and dinosaur pairings, and other people's boyfriends. And I guess, really, that's why I hate gay Asians. And I guess that's why I hate myself. Buster Tennyson Chang. Nice to meet you.

Wreck Beach

Kurt locks the car, extracts the key from its round nest. He tosses it up where it hovers, momentarily, catching a sharp glint of sunlight before it falls neatly into his palm. "Hey, come on!" He nods his head in the direction of the trail-head, picks up his stride.

Is he annoyed? I'm unsure. Kurt moves so quickly, I try not to mistake impatience for irritation. What else to do but follow: concentrate on nothing, the inside of boxes, the centre of Os? Sometimes, I focus on the rugged path in front of me, tumbling haphazardly down a steep slope of green trees and moss. I slap at mosquitoes. I lose thoughts in the motion of hands.

I've forgotten something though. I know I have. It took Kurt a swift ten minutes to pull out of his West End apart-ment's parking spot and show up at my building, poking at the intercom: three quick rings, always the same. I threw my stuff together and rushed out the door.

At the bottom of the path, I catch my breath, try to let the sweat from the walk dry off. I take off my shoes and look around. It's a bright, almost cloudless day. The beach is crowded: volleyball nets and sun umbrellas, baskets of food and suntan lotion, a jostling sea of nude bodies. A woman, naked except for a money belt, sells sushi from a tray suspended at her waist. Someone else is selling vodka popsicles. All this unlicensed vending adds even more of an illicit appeal.

I scan the beach and notice Marliss off to the left, out of calling distance but easily spotted, that wild frizz of hair and her hot pink beach towel. "You drop your drawers, strip off your bra, we're all the same! Toss your shorts, toss your labels!" That's what she told me the first time we came to Wreck Beach together. She's the unofficial tidal princess here, the regular of all regulars, one of the devoted. People cram together as if on a huge church picnic. Believers blessed with light against a backdrop of blue. Other beaches have invisible barriers put up to keep each party in separate quarters. Not here. She looks up and waves cheerily. She doesn't like Kurt so I'll go and visit with her later.

Kurt walks some distance, stops, then snaps out his towel in one quick motion. I watch it hover, a displaced ocean wave.

"Hey, slowpoke!" says Kurt.

"Hot sand," I reply. It's my sandals I forgot.

As usual, he takes a long time to undress. Kurt doesn't believe in this equality in nudity business, which is why he reads the scene, scouts for muscles, V-shaped torsos, handsome jaw lines; things beyond what makes us all the same.

Us, meaning to Kurt men. Or gay men to be precise. His eyes magically filter out women, children, male-female couples and men who don't have the right haircut, walk, swimsuit.

I notice him doing a 180-degree scan and ask, "What do you think?"

"Possibilities," he replies.

~

Usually Kurt asks "how can you be so blind?" but today it's obvious. I often can't tell if someone is gay but it's easier when they're in clusters like this. I'd guess that the three young guys next to us with gym-fit bodies are in their twenties. The darkest one, maybe a Latino, is especially toned. This is why Kurt has chosen this spot. "For a bit of view," he might say if he told me what he was thinking. "Beauty equals vanity," I'd reply. Even to look at, I'd rather admire something more normal.

This whole world – dating, relationships, the scene – mystifies me. How can Kurt, after what we go through as gay men, be so confident? Where did he get that steady walk and hand? I've told him that I would have hated him if we'd met when we were younger: he more arrogant than he is now and me trying to climb out of self-consciousness.

Sometimes he shakes his head at me when I'm clumsy, that's the bad response. Or a little smile like we're sharing a joke, that's a good response. I've been waiting for four years for some of his assuredness to wear off on me but I'm not sure if it's happening.

My good qualities, ones I think Kurt could use a bit of: Patience. Sincerity. Modesty. It's good not to boast, that's what Mom always said. Once in a job interview, I was asked for ten of my good qualities. I broke into a sweat at four. My white dress shirt was soaked by the time they let me go.

"What do you see in me?" I ask Kurt. The reply is different each time, as if it's being thought up as we go along. This could be taken as a good sign.

"Do you want your back done?" I show him the tanning lotion in my hand.

"Later."

It's not so hot anyway, and he doesn't sunburn as easily as I do. I hear that in the southern hemisphere, where the ozone layer is thin, the sun gets you whether you can see it or not.

~

I lie back and try to get comfortable. Some people are beach people. I'm not but I pretend to be. If there's no wind, it's too hot. But a bit of wind makes sand fly into your eyes no matter what — from people drying themselves off, walking by, shifting around. And how do you tell the difference between healthy pink and on your way to a bad burn? Especially with sunglasses. When they're on, your skin is a different colour. When they're off, it's still not the right colour because your eyes are adjusting and squinting back to normal. I find it all a bit stressful.

The beach is a good place for thinking though, maybe because of the sound of the water. I recline and stretch out and find myself counting the number of times Kurt and I have split up and got back together. In four years: the time after the first affair; when we both got too busy at work; when his ex-boyfriend started leaving messages on my answering machine. Those were the big ones, though I have to say the make-up sex is great.

I guess it's that I'm used to him. I wear him like an old shirt, worn at the folds and inseam, but at least I know where the weak parts are and it has lasted so long, not like some others. At least I know him so well.

Which should make it easier, really, knowing that Kurt is interested in the Latino guy relaxing five feet over from us. No surprise. I can guess what he'll do.

"Lotion?"

"After a swim."

He'll stay in one spot for now, make himself conspicuous, a few quick glances. If he gets the right signal, he'll get up and do something. Swim, walk, whatever. I'd estimate fifteen minutes. The timing is consistent.

~

How did we get from him cruising me to him cruising other people in front of me? I review our history often. Sometimes, I consider that an alien has replaced me in all of this, or an evil twin has replaced him.

I didn't know what hit me the first time I met Kurt. I was alone at a club, waiting for a friend to show, pissed off since I hardly ever went out and couldn't believe I was being stood up. I decided to dance anyways and was drawn into his orbit, a sharp, energetic dancer with a white t-shirt, short hair, cute face. He looked at me then, right in the eyes. I got flustered and went to sit down but he followed me.

"Hi." Direct. "Listen, I can't stay tonight but I'd like to get to know you better. Can I get your phone number?"

Kurt, he recounts different things: the song by Bronski Beat, that he was in an aggressive mood and that he'd decided that night he would pick up. He tells our friends that I looked like a dancing want ad.

Last year, he came up with a proposal. "Look. Every time you find out I'm with someone else, we break up. And I don't want to break up and neither do you. It's just sex. After three years, it's still good, but I've got other needs that have to be met."

Needs to be met. Where have I heard that before? Real life or some trashy TV show? Why does the language of relationships always sound like you've heard it some other time?

Maybe I'm over-dramatising. He has, in fact, only picked someone up in front of me once, and it was because he thought he could make it seem like something else. The rest of the time, he's just being gregarious.

Still, I like it when it's just the two of us. I feel like a shiny coin, lost once but now chosen. I don't try to explain this to my friends.

Mr Latino has decided to take a swim. He stands up, a net of muscles unfolding down his torso. Walks to the shore with a friend, doesn't notice our attention. He's used to people looking at him. Kurt waits two, three minutes, brushes sand off his legs, and follows. He steps in, ignoring the cold, and moves out to where it's deeper. They're still wading in when he plunges in off to the left of them.

The other point to be made is that Kurt doesn't do it all that often. He even tells me about them – the one with the chest of a bear, the ones that talk too much. I like this. I find it interesting, at times unsettling, but mostly I feel like a confidante, a keeper of secrets. Of course, I'm supposed to sleep around as well. Which I've considered. But it doesn't really work for me.

We talked about it all the time for the first months after we made our "agreement". What was I going to tell people? What if the people he sleeps with meet me? What if he falls in love? How often did he do this before we made it official? I thought we could talk about it endlessly, but I was wrong. I got tired.

I did tell Marliss though what had happened, hoping to get a bit of sympathy. I had a broken arm once and thought it was the strangest thing how people on the street kept smiling and nodding at me.

"Agreement? Yeah, right." Then she launched into complaining about a pretentious co-worker, maybe because she'd been my confidante for the previous infidelities and she didn't want to hear any more. "But what about the first time?" She interrupted her own story to return to the topic. "You were so angry you didn't talk to him for a week."

I tell her that he's not jealous, so why should I be?

"That's because you don't have sex with other people. Is the rest of your relationship so good that you're going to put up with this?"

It was about this time that Marliss gave up pretending to like Kurt. Now, they don't talk to each other at all.

~

That water out there, salty and dark. What is it telling me? Can it wash away the litter in my head? Leave me with a clean bed of thoughts: sand, simple and sparkling. It looks too cold to jump in. The sun pins me in place and I can't move off this towel.

We must look like targets here. Seen from above: round, gaudy red-and-white beach umbrellas, feet sticking out below, or on our towels, flesh outlined in colourful stripes. There are targets down here too. My first visits to Wreck Beach, my eyes would only focus on what I'd always been told not to look at: pink nipple, triangle of pubic hair, dangly cock and balls. I got over the novelty, but you can still see the wonder on the faces of newcomers that come down to look and not look at the same time.

It's a skill this: seeing things without looking, developing sight in the corner of your eyes. I'm practising myself. Looking like I'm sleeping but watching Kurt swimming while the two other guys are chatting and paddling around over to the side. Ripples in the water spread out, touch each other and disappear.

We want it all, don't we? Independent but taken care of. Settled but able to explore. Married but able to screw around when we want to. I know I've got things I want. I want to be happy. I want Kurt. I want Kurt to be happy, so sometimes I let him do things that make me unhappy. Marliss calls me a wimp but I don't see her happy being single.

Kurt suddenly appears beside me, towelling off seawater. I must have dozed off.

"Hey, watch the water! You're getting me."

"Oh, sorry."

"Do you want to go pretty soon?"

"The water's nice today. You're not into a swim?" He drapes the towel on his shoulders, points off to the left where there's a rock ledge leading out into the ocean. "Are you going to stay here?"

I nod, yeah, and watch while he gets smaller and smaller.

There's a softball game in the distance. A ball is hit high into the air with a solid *thwack*. I try to follow it with my eyes but feel dizzy. Eleven is the last age I remember having a baseball glove on. My elementary school, like so many on the West Side named after a British lord: mine was Trafalgar. A tiny diamond, stuck in outfield, the ball climbing up and falling down again, in front of me in the sky, a small ugly planet.

Where is it going to land? Should I go forward, should I go backwards? I stumbled around in a circle and for one white second, thought I'd been hit by the ball because all the scenery had disappeared around me. But no, the ball had sailed over my head, a graceful arc. I turned around, thinking that if my mind was so strong that it could block out reality, why couldn't I have willed the softball right into the cradle of my outstretched glove? Or willed myself right out of the game?

Years later, when I'd finally discovered that I needed glasses, I remembered the soft lob of the pitch, the perfect hit by the batter, and the whole world out of focus. By that time, it was too late to learn to catch. When you're not a child and can't play ball, no one is going to teach you.

~

Thirty, maybe forty minutes later, I am looking for Kurt. Marliss and her crew have left already. We had a quick chat before she left, and I said I'd call her tonight. My skin is sticky with lotion and is imprinted with sand and my towel. I've spent too long in the sun. I look for pollen in the air, but only see that clouds have rolled in. The bridge of my nose is plugged with heat.

I don't see him, but the party next to us is getting ready to leave: lifting up towels, digging out clothes from a backpack. It's only the two friends though. Where's the Latino? I roll onto my stomach and then I see them, up near the trail entrance back to the road. They're talking together, casually, Kurt's arms loose behind his back. I notice that the Latino talks with his hands. He's partially clothed though, looks about to go. He leans over, reaches his hand out, touches Kurt lightly on the shoulder and turns to face his friends, mouths "shall we go?" Two nods of agreement. They head up to the trailhead. Kurt passes them on the way and smiles. He's taking his time though. When he arrives back here, he spreads out his towel. One brisk motion.

I guess we'll stay longer after all. The sun is less harsh,

it's becoming quieter and you can hear the waves if you concentrate. I don't ask what happened but Kurt tells me anyway.

"Daniel. From Toronto. Leaves tomorrow. Going to Denman Station tonight with friends, if we want to join him."

My mouth stalls in between catty responses. 'As if.' 'Why would I want to?' 'Oh, you go on and enjoy yourself.'

"Cute, huh? We were just talking." Making it sound like I'd implied something else when I haven't said anything at all. He shrugs his shoulders, half-smiles, lies back down.

I shrug too, an echo. On my back looking up, my hands behind my head, I play games with the clouds, look for shapes and figures. It's a leftover habit from childhood and I'm glad that some things don't change all that much. In the big puffy cloud overhead, I see ridges on a mountain. Also, whispers of clouds in thin streams, like ropes, or claws. I'm a climber on these hills swinging from uncertain lines of safety to grasp at others: danger, excitement, stupidity. I giggle at my melodrama. Kurt stirs, and I notice that he's falling asleep.

I'll wake him up soon. I'm not staying here forever. The sun is lower now, people are starting to hike up the main trail in pairs and small groups. Going home, or out to dinner, maybe to a night shift at work. Dispersing like clouds.

When in September I finally call it quits, I'll have no idea where the words have come from – TV, movies, a book. "This really isn't working for me." How will I find the strength to say it? Will something have finally rubbed off after all? “I mean it this time. Sorry.”

For now, Kurt is sleeping: legs stretched right out, chest rising and falling with each breath, his shirt loosely draped over his stomach and thighs. I’ve seen his face a thousand times but I study it again carefully. It’s neutral, a child-like peace. I don’t think he’s thinking of anything at all. I smile. When I close my eyes, I still see the sun, the brightness through the red of my eyelids.

Maintenance

I'm on my way to Saskatoon to see my best friend Carlo and I can't believe how cold it is outside. The weatherman says it's thirty-five below. Nothing I've ever experienced growing up. The grey highway streaked with white zooms by below, patterns of speed and shadow; the tinted windows, frosted and steamy, give the interior of the bus a dusky yellow glow. I'm groggy, excited, scared.

Have you ever had a best friend? I remember the concept before the reality, and even then, sitting on the stairs in the empty elementary school, it was an admission: "I guess I don't have a better friend than you."

Logic dictated, therefore, that we were best friends, me and Clive Perry, the squeaky-voiced son of two Salvation Army missionaries. He moved away a short year after.

I still remember the crumpled ball feeling in my heart at his letter imploring me to accept Jesus into my life. He worried about my imminent descent to hell.

Things like this made me a little wary of the world. No poverty, abuse, divorce, or deaths in the family, but I was an odd, vulnerable child. I could sense that I was different from others, and knew that would lead to difficulties. Somehow, I felt as if made of glass, and whatever it was I really wanted slid off my surfaces. Nothing could grab hold.

The weather here in Saskatchewan is similar: ungrippable, so cold you can't open your hand to grab at the air. At rest stops, we madly dash into the fluorescent-lit diners. I'm surprised at the physical pain of it all, a prairie winter like a wall of needles.

~

On the bus from Vancouver, I snuggle into my jacket and stretch out in peace. *I don't have to ask permission when I want to go out fishin'*, Tom Waits growls from my Walkman, . . . *better off without a wife*. Earlier, a young woman who boarded in Kamloops sat beside me and talked, unconcerned whether I was interested or not, not noticing my perfunctory interjections were no more than a mumble.

She told me her life story, or many life stories: "I have a brain tumour and doctors tell me they don't know how long I'll live. It's why I can't eat pizza because fat foods make me dizzy even though pizza's my favourite food in the whole world. Which is why my boyfriend tried to choke me, there are marks to prove it."

All the way to Saskatoon, I fall into these intimate stories of a stranger – the recent suicide of a friend, a broken home, hospital operations. But how intimate are they if not all of them are true? Light from the tinted windows coloured her face, the motor's vibration seeped into my bones. True or not, I liked the way she improvised her history. I liked the way she showed me that whatever I believe is true are probably just crazy stories to her too.

Carlo is a story, one I'll keep short rather than long. I think we all have people in our lives, or at least I hope we do, that make us gasp in surprise at how well they knew us before they even met us, at how we can't imagine not knowing each other.

Carlo and I met while at an international school in Vancouver. He was all the way from Costa Rica; I was a local, more or less. Abbotsford was too close to be considered foreign, but far enough away that I stayed in the dormitories with all the others. I was fascinated by anything different from my home town or even Vancouver, which I was beginning to consider comfortable but not all that exciting. Carlo represented a whole world that I knew nothing about.

We were not philosophers together, nor workers, we did not run to each other like sisters in times of trouble, nor gossip like village neighbours. In fact, we did not see each other that much more than other friends, and we were not possessive or jealous of each other's time. But when we did catch up over a hot chocolate or an illicit beer, there was an understanding and warmth, good acoustics like a grand piano on a stage, lit from above, echoes around the warm wooden hall. A song that is both familiar and unknown that hovers around you but does not demand you, you can sink into its round bright tones or slide away so that the notes become a background of evening stars.

I had no logical reason to believe I could trust Carlo with the biggest secret of my life. In fact, he'd never met anyone gay in Costa Rica where he grew up and his parents had told him that homosexuals were criminals and drug users. But I trusted him, and the words "I'm gay" were starting to consume me from the inside out. What I didn't know was how he would react. In the school's amphitheatre, the two of us sat alone cross-legged on the stage, my hands shaking and my breath uneven.

He listened to me. His dark eyes met mine. His voice did not catch. He admitted that he was shocked but said that he would never walk away from me. The wonderful bravado and drama of youth. And he did not walk away.

I learned something from him and his Latin friends. It's a subjective view, of course: Canadians are a kind, gentle people but reserved. At worst, reserved like a table can be reserved with four empty seats in a crowded restaurant. You know that the little sign on the tabletop means you're in for disappointment and that you'll have to find another place to eat.

These young men and women from Argentina and Bolivia, Chile and Mexico, they could lift their hips into rhythm that a Northerner could only dream of, they could lift the corners of their hearts like a smile, or let loose a tear-shaped wail, or a jalapeño pepper scream. At least that's what I thought at the time, and still do, sometimes.

A wonderful painter with dancing eyes named Rosita told me "I love you" and it all fell into place. For a young Canadian to tell his friend "I love you" means many things. "I have known you for a long time and feel a deep affection for you"; "You can count on me if you need me"; "Your friendship means so much to me that I can say these dangerous intimate words." But for a beautiful Colombian girl to tell this to me, without romantic intentions, meant, simply, "I love you." The emotions were pure and warm. Granted, they may last five minutes or five years, but the words I heard were much different from what I was used to. I appreciated the difference.

~

I don't know whether I was in love with Carlo in the usual sense. I know there was a deep connection, some chain of gold at the bottom of the sea. I do remember being inconsolably sad when we parted. He wrote to me later that he'd felt much the same.

Our last night together, we talked late into the evening. I promised to visit him one day in Costa Rica, "maybe for your wedding," I joked and imagined myself as best man. Carlo was in my room to sleep over the night, but when we were tired, he did not lie down on the extra mattress. Our eyes met, he nodded and we slid under the covers of my slim single bed. I guess I wanted to hold and be held that last night, not knowing when we'd see each other again. But Carlo curled into himself, arms folded over his chest and turned away. I rubbed his back as he fell asleep, then masturbated as quickly and silently as I could.

Don't get me wrong. My hand was sticky but my mind was clear: I did not want to keep him, I did not want him to be my boyfriend, I did not want to have sex, I knew he was straight and had a girlfriend. But I knew that I was happy to be his best friend and that for the five minutes or five days or the last five months that we had been together, my intimacy had reached a point that without being sexually attracted to him, the passion had risen within me and on that last night together, found release.

Or maybe I was just another horny teenager. We woke up, tangled against the wall, skin touching.

Carlo's girlfriend when I'd met him was a round-faced Ecuadorian girl named Luisa. We all spent some time together, and though Luisa and I didn't have much to say to each other, we enjoyed each other's company. I liked that they didn't treat me like a third wheel. I had seen couples fall in love and retreat into a cocoon, to return only with vacant expressions, and distant eyes the colour of daylight. Luisa and Carlo stayed present.

Once Luisa had asked Carlo if he had a best friend. He had said no, and then later returned to her with my name. "Of course," said Luisa. Her inseparable best friend was Giovanna who she turned to when Carlo broke up with her.

Lara is another story. She was also from far away though not as far as the foreign students. Ice-bound Saskatoon, Saskatchewan. The non-Canadians loved the sound of that. "Oh, stop exaggerating. It's not always that cold." But none of us believed it, imagining snowshoes and frost.

She was a good friend, made better by the fact she was in a relationship with my best friend. We were in English class together and had picked each other out as potential allies the very first week of class. She showed me Atwood's *Surfacing*, which I took in like snow absorbs sound; I rushed to show her Kundera's *Laughable Loves*, which repelled her even though she loved his language. "But what a sexist pig! All those women as objects!"

She approached me to have coffee with her a month or two after Carlo and she had started "going out." The relationship between Carlo and Lara was young, so I understood she was nervous. But I knew Carlo was smitten with Lara.

"But all the girls are interested in him. And he's so charming. It always seems like he's flirting with them."

I joked with her, or started to before I saw how serious she was.

"I just can't trust him, Sam. I can't go any further in this."

What to do? In my best counselling voice I said, "Lara, he's my best friend and I know he likes you. I'm sure he's being honest with you about how he feels."

"I know, but I just can't. I can't." She looked utterly unconvinced, tear ducts on red alert.

"Sometimes you just have to let go, you know? You just have to begin." I put down my tea, stared at her and said "Let me tell you a story about trust."

Maybe I realised that I was growing up too, since it was the first time I had told someone I was gay without the point of the story being that I was gay: it was just part of the story I was telling. While I would have many more momentous coming-outs ahead of me, it was a start, that story. A telling where sexuality took a supporting role to the starring role of Carlo, finishing with appropriate hero dialogue: "I won't walk away."

Lara looked up, dazed, quiet, and left the room. The next time I saw her, she was together with Carlo, happy, laughing and falling in love.

I've only told you part of the story so far. The other part which I soon learned was that part of the bountiful gracious love that Carlo gave to me was not to be separated from the rest of his personality, a romantic that would die for love, and die for his friends. But love comes first.

Carlo and Lara didn't know exactly what would happen at their parting, but they were both far too deeply in love to let anything get in their way. They both left for their home towns, and I accepted a place at Queen's University in Kingston, Ontario. During breaks from his studies at San Jose University, Carlo would bus, or train, or occasionally fly back to cold Saskatoon to find warmth in love's arms. When Lara finished her studies for the summer, she would do the reverse journey, a migration to the south, long hot summers in Costa Rica with Carlo and his family. Three years together since entering university and they managed to spend at least four months of every year together. Not bad for long-distance love.

And what did I get while they were dying of love, that dangerous burning while together, those painful months apart and budget-shattering phone bills? I wrote to Carlo regularly for the first year, a bit less regularly the next. Long letters, with poems and thoughts, stories about coming out to parents and friends, about looking for a relationship and not finding it: one false start and a heart tired of being patient all the time. I had the occasional liaison but these I usually didn't write about. The full romantic history would have to wait until we could catch up in person. Occasionally I would receive a hand-written letter back (mine were always typed) that sometimes but often did not correspond to my letters, meaning that some had been missed along the way and gone to the great Costa Rican post office in the sky.

One summer, I got a phone call from Lara who asked if her cousin visiting the west coast could stay with me in Abbotsford on his way to Vancouver. I said yes, though he never showed up in the end.

"How's Carlo?" I asked, a bit anxious, maybe annoyed, trying not to seem neglected. It had probably been about a year at that time since I'd heard from him and while I knew that quality of a friendship does not necessarily relate to quality of correspondence, I missed him. I occasionally felt pangs of emotion, like an egg in a frying pan, the edges beginning to burn, a sense of something that could appease the senses but could also go badly awry.

"Oh, Carlo? He's doing really well. I hear from him at least once a week, sometimes more. What? He still hasn't written to you? Listen, I'll make sure that he writes to you when I go and see him. I promise, OK?"

I hung up the phone and heard a tinkling sound like a broken filament in a light bulb. Or imagined myself that bulb, burnt out and blackened, unusable. I decided that as soon as possible, I would try to see Carlo again before it was too late.

~

It took a few seasons for the timing to be right. I was home for Christmas in Abbotsford; Carlo was with Lara for the winter in Saskatoon. I'd arranged far in advance that I would leave on Boxing Day and visit them on my way back to Kingston.

Now, I'm almost off the bus, wondering what my stories will sound like when lifted from the page and the words are released into fleshy daylight, when I'll get to tell him in person what I've written in the letters, the ones that arrived and the ones that disappeared.

When I arrive, I look like all the other passengers, disoriented, a cramped fatigue suddenly released into open space. Carlo sees me first, and I hear the footsteps running, open my arms into an embrace. Happy and nervous.

"You look older, something about your face."

"Do I?" and now he studies mine, "I guess you look different too." We hop into a van that Lara's family has given him to drive for the duration of his stay. We zoom off to the house, exhaust hitting the freezing air, rising up and disappearing into white blue.

"I'm sorry I haven't written to you more. I'm loving medical school, but it's taking every minute of my time."

We chatter, small talk, remembering the sound of each other's voices. Carlo is having a good visit; Lara's dad is a doctor too and they talk trade. Lara's mom, a potter, takes good care of them and gives them space. Lara is happy though busy with school.

As we drive, I wonder about the time between us. When people talk of school friends and university friends, what does it mean? There is a North American college experience that is different than in other parts of the world. The young leave their homes and travel to one place. They live in close proximity, and their basic needs – food, accommodation – are taken care of. They can explore, if inquisitive, tomes upon tomes filled with different types of thinking and ideas. There is all the time in the world to learn about oneself and to spend with others. Out of this, friendships form.

After this rite of passage, where do you go with your fellow travellers? Settle into more sedentary lives, reminisce about the past when meeting again? With more experience, how much do we change? Does all this new information attach itself physically to our bodies? Impossible then to snap back together like jigsaw puzzle pieces?

Lara greets me with a friendly hug and takes my backpack. I look around to see a beautiful house belonging to a doctor and an artist with paintings all around and bookshelves filled with ceramic treasures. We chat in the kitchen, waiting for the kettle to boil, fill each other in on missing facts and details. Lara pulls Carlo towards her, rubs her foot against his as she talks.

The cartoonist Eric Orner calls it one of the seven deadly sins of love: couples that cling to each other while talking to you. I wonder if I'm imagining things but no, this is evident enough. It's Lara who can't keep off him. He may be a willing participant, but it is her arms that grab and pull, her leg reaching over to slide up his pantleg, her hand reaching up into his dark hair and stroking his skull as we talk about the most mundane things, what to eat for dinner, how the weather might change.

I'm impatient, so many questions to ask, but the day unfolds at a leisurely pace: dishes to do, meals to prepare. My face neutral but inside, I struggle against anxiety. Even warming up the car in this frigid weather takes time. And

I'm disoriented too. I've never been in weather like this where nature sets the rules. Everything slows down two steps. My Kingston winters are not nearly as cold.

The next days are the same and I watch the calendar. Three days gone, four days left. This is not the same as before. The geography has changed. The gift of time at international school has expired and life at this phase takes up so much time. I've scarcely had a moment to talk with Carlo and we're always together, the three of us. I start to plot a way of getting time with him alone.

New Year's Eve. Lara's parents are off to a party. Her mother stops for a moment before leaving: "Isn't New Year's Eve the perfect time to wear this feather boa?" I decide that I like her quite a bit more than I do Lara. She floats out the door. "Have fun!"

We settle down to share a quiet dinner and a bottle of wine, listen to music and talk as the hours roll by, readying to break open a bottle of champagne. Carlo gives me a big hug at the stroke of midnight, a longer one to Lara, and Lara and I exchange a friendly embrace.

Carlo and I stay up a little while longer as Lara prepares downstairs to go to bed. I tell him a story about a big party in Kingston where I got drunk on sake. We reminisce about a time when we did the same together in Vancouver, under-age and drunk for one of the first times. "I wish you were there, Carlo."

He's hit by this, his eyes well up.

"Carlo, we're not having enough time to talk. I've got so much to tell you."

"I don't know how you picked me. Out of all the incredible people there are in the world." He looks away for a beat, and returns. "I have a lot to tell you too. About my relationship with Lara, about everything. Things have changed."

It is at that moment that Lara calls from the bedroom, and I meet Carlo's eyes. "She can't sleep without me," he mouths, and slips away. "We'll talk tomorrow."

~

Tomorrow comes, and tomorrow is the day I've chosen. I keep my plans silent for now, like a doctor hiding in his lab coat. The day passes much the same as the days before. I wait until evening. I follow them to their bedroom just after Carlo has gone in and knock on the door. Lara looks surprised. She's half-sitting up, looks around and then arranges the covers around her waist, expectantly.

"I want to talk to you both for a while tonight." I sit down, awkward, shy. "I want to ask if I can spend the day with Carlo tomorrow." There's silence and no reply so I continue: "Not just a bit of the day, but the whole day. Maybe go out to lunch and dinner, go dancing at a . . . club." A gay club, I mean to say, but I can't. I want him to see a part of my life that is different than before.

"I'm really feeling that Carlo is not going to enjoy himself with me, or in fact, any time away from you, unless you say it's OK." *How did it come to this?*

"I don't think you understand," she cuts in, "and I don't think it's something that we can reason through."

"You knew I was coming. Surely I can have some time."

"Lara has been making time for you. She's saved all her studying for when you'd be here."

"But Carlo, we haven't had one late-night conversation. You're always being called off to her side."

"But Lara can't fall asleep unless I'm there. I told you that. I can't let her stay up like that."

"But what does she do when you're not here? What do you do, Lara," I turn to her, "when he's not here? Surely you can use whatever it is that gets you through that?"

"But he is here. Right here."

Silence. But a noisy silence like in a waiting room. I suddenly remember the conversation years ago between Lara and me, a gift of trust and believing it a starting point to Lara and Carlo's new relationship. Give it back to me, I think, looking at her.

I pull out my final card. "I've been working with assumptions for the last few years, assumptions that Carlo is my best friend and that I am his. You've managed to spend so much time together in the last years. I haven't seen him for three years and I'm here for one week. I'm asking for a day, Lara. I have to believe that I'm worth that time or else I have to start rearranging the world that these assumptions are based upon . . ." I falter, I was never very good at speeches. They see my hands curved upwards as if attempting to catch some lost promise.

"We've got something special, Sam. You know that, why don't you understand?"

"You own him heart and soul, forever. I'm here for a few days. I'm gay, Lara. All that time when I was alone in college and didn't know anyone else who was gay, Carlo gave me his acceptance. He gave me his friendship. Does that mean nothing to you?"

"I know but . . . It's him too, it's him."

"I know." I know that Carlo wants this.

"If there's anyone in the world who I want to understand this, it's you," says Carlo. "It doesn't mean you're not my best friend. It's been three years since you've last seen us together and it's different now."

Lara continues. "We've had to fight to make this last, and I don't want to spend time apart from him. It may seem a long time to you but it's not, and I want to be with Carlo every single moment."

The drama of youth. Or is it just plain selfishness, or is it me, the selfish one?

"Surely just one day after so many years."

"No, I can't! Any other time of the year is different, but when I'm with Carlo, I don't see my friends, I don't see my family. This is the way we've had to be to make this survive and I'm not willing to change it."

"It's different when we're here," says Carlo. "Lara's

parents let us sleep together but when we're home in Costa Rica, we have to be apart every night."

"It's just not the same," says Lara, exasperated.

Of course I understand what she is saying. It's just that I won't accept it. Love has different rules, she says plainly, in many words, or none. It is on her face. And I reply without words as well: I do not have love. I refuse to be locked out of this world.

"I know it's not the same," I answer in the same tone, "but I thought you understood what Carlo means to me. I'm not the same as your other friends. I haven't had the same chances for relationships as you, I couldn't. This society hates so much. I could only have friends, and that's where I found the love and acceptance I needed."

I am embarrassed at having revealed so much. "And Carlo has been my best friend. We have so much shared history." I'm crying now, and look at Lara through this watery shield.

"I don't want to be mean," she says.

"I know," I look at her face lit from behind by the bedside lamp. She is not looking at me but instead at Carlo, emotional and unemotional, fatigued, steady. Carlo stares silently between us, finds no middle ground, and stares into empty space, confused, slightly desperate, though the storm has passed.

I decide that night that I will leave for Kingston as soon as I can, the morning after tomorrow. The next day, Lara feels sick, so sick that I do have the whole day to spend with Carlo after all, driving around Saskatoon in the cold.

In the van with Carlo, I can't bring myself to tell him how much I was hurt that he never stood up for me, that he never gave me that time himself, the time I wanted, the time I believed would allow us to continue being best friends. That best friends, gay or straight, come in second place.

I won't see Carlo again for another three years. By that time, the relationship will not have worked out and Carlo will explain to me that he never knew why Lara didn't like me, but that she didn't, and didn't like it when he talked about me.

I'll ponder about best friends and friendship, and decide that we were best friends for a time, and no longer are. While I don't rule out the possibility of other people having best friends for life, I rule out the possibility for me and know that it is not Carlo's or Lara's or my fault but that sometimes the models we imagine don't work out.

And that night? I step out of the bedroom, walk up to the main floor, the tears finding their way again. I find a low chair and slump into it. I know I can make the crying stop, think of something absurd, or simply not think. But I want these weighty sobs.

I walk slowly through the living room, into the kitchen. Next to the stairs on a coat rack is a stethoscope belonging to Lara's father. I reach out, stretch open its metal arms and place the ends in my ears. The fabric of my shirt blocks the sound so I slip the cold metal disk gingerly under my shirt, place it on the skin near my heart, and shut my eyes.

Yes, it is beating, an organic irregular thump, not a metronome, nor a clock. The spaces in between fill with a great cavernous sound, an inner ocean, the interior of shells. I want to be that, what I'm listening to: dark, earthy red, dynamic, unthinking. Unconscious but full of life.

"Steady." I put the stethoscope back in place and slip upstairs to sleep.

Calendar Boy

January

It's the images. Men made into statues. Perfectly expressionless faces. Bodies like he's never seen before, set in the softest edge of shadow, in the afterthought of light; amidst tropical jungles or northern forests, overexposed beaches, hidden lakes; decorated in water frozen in mid-air, beads of sweat in complicated patterns.

What fascinates him the most is the body divided into sections – like window panes or puzzle pieces or the day's boxes on a calendar month. When he focuses in on these smaller parts, he loses the bigger picture, sees new details, worlds within worlds he's never noticed.

Like the lines dividing the body, their tension wrapping around the form. If you could somehow untie the knots that hold these lines together, would the rope simply fall away, a Houdini escape trick, the shadows of pectoral and torso and the web of abdominal muscles disappearing and leaving a more formless shape? Gods become human again, arms unencumbered by large bumps and lines, a smooth flat back rather than a mountainous landscape.

Or are these lines of definition actually holding something back? If released, would the body spring out, become fat? A larger version finally free?

Gary knows that in his case, he'd be back to where he started. Shorter. Thinner. Not that he could do anything about his height. A gym buddy told him it's probably to his advantage. If he was tall, it might take forever for him to fill out, rather than the quick progress Gary's achieved: arms, chest, thighs, all expanding. But skinny, yeah, if he stopped working out, if the lines disappeared, that's what he'd return to.

So, which calendar will he choose? The black-and-white ones are more classy than the ones in colour, with their slightly lurid bright shades of flesh and swimsuits. The bodybuilder one he skips over too; Gary likes muscles but these guys are ridiculous. Another with couples he also rejects. Why would you want to look at two men in states of lust when you're single yourself? Salt in the wound and all that. A military theme: no. Latino men: no. A few of the models are beautiful but he doesn't want to be that limited.

He finally settles on the one with black-and-white photography, models all very well-defined and muscular, only a few too big. The title of this one is *Desire* and even though most of the model's body is in view in each photo, you can clearly see the facial expressions, sultry and come-hither, eyes direct into the camera, variations on a theme.

Gary pays at the counter, feeling sweaty and overheated, and hopes that his roommate won't be home when he gets back to the apartment.

February

All February, Gary works out. If he's short of time, he'll go to the university recreation centre, but mainly he goes to the YMCA downtown, where there are more people. He does his sets, and scans the room in between. He hopes no one notices him watching.

It's a good month to work out hard; it's cold and damp and grey. What else is there to do? Business classes crawl along. Though at least he's learning something: setting goals, strategic planning, working towards an end result, measuring the achievements.

He uses his calendar at home to mark his progress: writes *Chest* and *Arms* in some boxes, *Legs* and *Back* in others. *Abdominals* are every day, they go in each box. He's bought a tape measure too, one that tailors use, although he doesn't record the results just yet. His chest seems different each day depending on how much he can inhale, and which part of his back the tape seems to rest on.

March

All month, Gary notices changes. Swelling in his body, more curve and breadth than ever before. His wardrobe changes too as he decides to stop wearing loose rugby shirts and long-sleeve business shirts. Make space for the tight white t-shirts, which he irons to a crisp sheen. The close fitting black Levi 501s. He notices eyes like never before: sidelong glances on the street, bolder stares in the clubs and bars.

In response, Gary walks upright, moves with a slower and more deliberate pace, and strides with legs slightly wider apart. He's even been treated like a bimbo. A *him*bo, he thinks, over for dinner at a friend's place. Mark's roommate couldn't stop staring at his chest, could only ask questions about his routine at the gym. Suddenly, his conversations were moving onto a different plane – guys asking him where he *worked out*, instead of simply where he *worked*. It all felt a bit easier.

Easier than at the meetings he's been going to lately, the city's gay Asian group. His first meeting, Chen, the president, a lawyer from Hong Kong, greeted him and asked "Do you speak Chinese?" Such a look of incredulity and pity at Gary's answer. Also, Chen and a few others broke into a long conversation in Cantonese during the middle of the meeting. Didn't they think it was rude that the rest of them couldn't understand?

But he goes to the meetings when he can. Something inside him says that it's the right thing to do. As well, he likes that the group's members are noticing his changes. No one else comes close to looking like him.

April

Gary's never approached anyone in a bar before. Men are always in tight clusters of friends; the ones who are alone usually radiate *need*, a dangerous energy. Tonight is different. All the compliments he's been getting lately, glances from random strangers through shop windows, in the mirrors at the gym: Gary feels desired.

The muscular blond with cheekbones and short hair *had* seemed to look at him near the bar's entrance, and again as they passed each other on the way to the restroom. He's not looking now from where he's leaning against the bar, but it's not an unfriendly expression on his face.

One of the guys at the meeting last month was talking about sex with bodybuilders. "You can never tell," he'd explained. "Two guys, both the same shape, the muscles might feel like sourdough bread, or they might feel like oak. You can't know by looking."

Bread or oak? Gary takes slow steps over. What will they talk about? At worst, polite conversation with an uninterested party. Or they'll talk about what they're doing, or where they're from. Or maybe they'll really like each other and just start talking. He glances at his watch and sees, with a jitter of nervousness, that it's almost closing time. Not perfect timing, but he's not going to pass this up.

Gary walks straight to the space at the bar next to him and orders a Coke. He didn't plan on doing this but he gets his drink, swings around to face away from the bar. Notices the blond glance at him, but so quickly he can't respond. "Hi," says Gary but the blond doesn't seem to notice him. Maybe the music is too loud. He shifts his weight onto his other foot. "Hi," a little louder, completely unprepared for the response: a slow turn of the head, a direct look in the eye, and not a change in pose, right elbow casually against the bar, left hand flat against the front of his thigh.

"No."

"Sorry . . . I . . ." backs away too quickly, *but I didn't ask a question,* Gary thinks. Sees a black space at the back of the man's throat, an illusion since the bar makes it too dark to see. But still this opening, pitch black, the belly of a coal mine, the centre of a deep forest. Echoing with the round and swirling shape of nothingness. O.

No.

May

He thinks about it for days, weeks. Works out harder under the theory: more action, less thought. But it comes back. Things Gary might have said. Excuses the blond might have had. Maybe he thought Gary was just trying to pick him up at the end of the night. Or, the looks exchanged earlier that night weren't looks at all but warnings to stay away.

The more he thinks about it, the more he's convinced it's something else. He's seen them in the gym, the white muscle boys together, all tall and the same shape, discussing clubs and dinner parties. He's felt them staring through him, not acknowledging his presence even when they're feet away from the weights he's using. At a guess, he figures they've worked out daily for years, and have probably dabbled in steroids. Some of their faces are taut and drawn, scarred with acne, a common side-effect, he's heard.

He thinks too of the models in the ads of the local gay newspaper, and then he thinks of all the models that he's seen, in magazines, gay or straight. When has he seen an Asian man as an object of desire, as part of a club, the club of people who fall in love and lust and have sex with each other? Rarely in movies, never on TV, not in the porn magazines he quietly flipped through in bookshops. Not on greeting cards, not in calendars . . .

June

Pink is a little too obvious, yellow, a bad joke. He considers blue, but decides in the end on red. It's an Asian colour, all those red envelopes and lanterns and tablecloths in Chinese restaurants.

Here's what it says:

> *Looking for hot Asian men to pose for a calendar. Masculine, athletic, straight-acting. Show us what you've got. Don't be shy.*

Then: contact information, address and phone number. He's printed and cut out 200 flyers, a little ambitious maybe, but then again, the Pride march is the city's biggest event. The crowds have already started to gather. Gary is dressed in a tiny pair of white shorts and black boots. Simple but effective, he hopes. Everyone's in a good mood, they thank him before reading the flyer he's just handed them.

He spots another head of black hair, and then is disappointed. It's Derek, this academic type from the gay Asian group. He doesn't trust him. Gary's arm hangs out with the flyer in mid-space, not wanting to give it to Derek, not able to hide it.

"Straight acting, what's that supposed to mean? I bet they don't look straight when they're down on their knees."

"Don't you know what I mean?"

"No." This queeny voice. Skips off, *ta-tah!* No, of course, he wouldn't know what it means.

July

Before the photo shoot, Gary works out extra hard, and without meaning to, skips meals. By the time he gets to Kenneth's house and the makeshift studio set up in his living room and backyard, Gary feels lean, toned, pumped up. He's had a workout an hour before just to make sure.

Kenneth is a friend of a friend, a photographer with a whole portfolio of photos of friends and acquaintances in grotesque poses, with fake blood and toy weapons as props. His art school efforts aren't paying the rent; fashion photography is. He's agreed to shoot Gary for free.

The high fence in the backyard obscures the view of neighbours, at least Gary hopes so, shivering slightly though the weather is warm, his naked skin glowing white against an overgrown maple tree. 'Should have gotten a bit of a tan,' he thinks as Kenneth asks him to stand, lie, kneel.

It's not long before he eases into comfort in front of the camera lens. Kenneth asks Gary to start with his underwear on. After the initial shots, he removes them though his genitals will be artfully hidden in the final shots. For now, it's easy to simply follow Kenneth's directions, keep a neutral expression on his face, concentrate on keeping his muscles tensed.

Inside, with blackout curtains over the window, Gary basks in the hot light of a theatre spotlight, Kenneth's prize from a recent garage sale. With the light angled down towards him, shadows form under his chest and in the crevices of his stomach. He thinks of the calendar, of himself in the calendar. No difference between him and the models in other calendars, the boys in the gym and the bars.

When the photos finally come back, Gary feels explosions of excitement all over his body. He can't believe his eyes. He knows it's him in the photos, the one who did all the posing and waiting. But the lighting and shadows make his body look like nothing he recognises. The chest is bigger, the muscles more defined, his face, too, is leaner, chin more angular, the face that people call boyish is more of a man's here.

Photos lie. Or do they? Is this a different person, a creation, is it trick photography? Or is it the best that Gary can be, the perfect man inside of him revealed on shiny paper. The men in the glossy men's exercise magazines, or fashion or porno mags: maybe they look a bit like him in real life. Or is it the other way around, that he looks a bit like them? No matter, he's excited about this project, maybe more excited than he's been for anything.

August

By the deadline, Gary has received four photos. One completely stunning Chinese Malaysian boy: how did he get so tall? A handsome Japanese man, and a compactly muscled Thai. He also received a photo of an entirely ordinary Chinese guy. Doesn't even look like he works out. Nude too. *Agh!* What was he thinking?

Four is enough to make a start, five including Gary, and if all else fails, maybe they'll have six models with two months each. *Which months would Gary choose?* No time to think about that, he's running through the presentation in his mind: upbeat, positive, and most of all, convincing.

"I've even got the title," he pauses for effect. "*Fresh Blood*!" Looks around at the nine guys in the room. "I know there's a market for this, even girls that I know, white and Asian, have said they'd love a calendar of hot Asian men."

"Is that the community we're aiming at?" It's Derek, dressed in a Greenpeace t-shirt, not even tucked in. Torn blue jeans. He doesn't add any more to the question, just leaves it hanging there.

"Well, no. Yes. We want to sell all the copies we produce, and we should sell them to anyone who appreciates it." Unsure if he's said the right thing. "But of course, the primary market is gay men."

"And does it say *gay* anywhere on the calendar?"

"No. We don't want to alienate anyone in the marketplace and limit our sales. It's evident. Who else buys these calendars? The models in the other ones are all gay too." Maybe reaching too hard with this one.

"Listen. I seriously think we need to consider if we would be buying into the commodification of the gay male, the reduction of ourselves to images of the body and our accompanying dehumanisation in the process. Aren't we aping the misogynistic hyper-masculine values that a heterosexist dominant society celebrates?" Derek scans the room piercingly.

Gary's left in a half-smile trying to figure out if anyone

else in the room understood what Derek just said. It doesn't look like it, since there's an air of confusion, and no one speaks.

Graham, overweight with heavy-framed glasses, pipes up from the corner. "Are you sure this is a sound idea financially? I don't think that community organisations are very good at selling merchandise. Remember the t-shirt fiasco two years ago?"

Gary looks over to President Chen hoping he'll be supportive, who instead says, "Let's hear from some others. Who else has something to add to the discussion?"

"I like the idea." Dear sweet William, a cute Vietnamese guy, with a light melodic accent. "We need more images of Asian beauty in the gay community. I'm tired of all the white men." He turns to Gary. "Can I help choose the models?"

September

He gets a phone call from Chen, thinks it's going to be about organising next month's "Korea Night" dance. But no, Chen's the bearer of bad news, as he puts it in an overbearing paternal sort of way. A little over-caring. But also the voice of reason. Gary can picture them all "discussing" the issue and then all looking towards Chen, meaning, you're the president, you get to do the dirty work.

"It's not necessarily a bad idea," the voice intones. "And

we appreciate the initiative shown and the new idea." We, as if it's the Communist Party or something. "It's just that we don't feel that we have the resources to fully support the project." Short pause. "And some concerns were raised about whether this is really the right message that we want to get across to the community."

October

It's rainy October, the city falling into depression, Gary is too. He's walking home from class and decides that it might help to stop in Flaunt, the newish bookstore on Dolan Street: brightly lit, stylish, and lots of gift items alongside books and magazines.

Gary is surprised. Only October and there are calendars out for the New Year. A tiny knot suddenly at the top of his stomach, he moves closer. Long-haired Chippendales, plastic skin and bodies; the slightly menacing but sexy Colt models, all hair and muscle and moustache; various porn star promos; shirtless firemen; a mostly clothed group of policemen, and numerous arty black-and-whites of identical white hairless men.

The next calendar would be a relief if it wasn't for the jealousy enveloping him, as if he'd set off the sprinkler system above with the heat from his anger. It's entitled *Asia*. Simple name, although it's a misnomer: one part of Asia only, the little finger deciding it's the whole hand. A benefit for an AIDS organisation in Hong Kong, it doesn't say gay anywhere, as if it needed to, twelve sepia photos of Chinese models in various states of nudity, backdrops of urban jungle – concrete lines of office towers and staircases. A big calendar, professional, glossy.

He won't buy it. No, definitely not. Words filling up the space above his head as if he's suddenly been drawn into the box of a comic strip: *scooped, beaten to the punch, to the finish line.* My idea. Damn those skinny politically correct geeks!

November

Classes this month focus on marketing and promotion, small business, and business plans. Gary follows them half-heartedly; he's still sore about the whole calendar incident. He looks at the box of photos, unused, that Kenneth took – in the backyard against the maple tree, lying in the leaves and grass, the indoor shot with dramatic lighting bringing shadows to the muscles in his chest and stomach. Such beautiful pictures. He hates wasting things, thinks he got that from his parents who never threw anything away. Rubber bands, stationery, nails and screws, old letters . . .

Greeting cards! He can get the negatives from Kenneth, investigate the art supply store for paper stock and envelopes. By that evening, he's worked out a list with six stores to approach, the names of printers, a rough schedule, a script: *"local entrepreneur . . . new consumer tastes . . . multiculturalism . . . tasteful . . . erotic."*

December

From a book on Chinese traditions, Gary remembers numbers.

Lucky number nine.

One hundred gates.

One thousand poems.

Four horsemen who saved China.

A five-toed imperial dragon.

Four auspicious events in the last month of a year.

The first event:

"Yes?"

"Gary, it's Chen. I know you haven't been to meetings for a while but we've got a favour to ask you."

"Uh huh."

"During the last meeting Derek led a discussion on racism, media representation and self-esteem."

"Uh huh."

"Well, the guys examined all fifty-two covers of last year's *Q Pink News* and they found that all of the cover boys were white except a black guy in March and two or three models who looked vaguely Latino, though they're probably Italian."

"And?"

"And they're protesting to the editor and have nominated you as a model for an upcoming cover. They figured you wouldn't mind . . . Gary?"

"Well . . ." Almost speechless. "You could have asked me first . . ."

The second: the cards are in three shops. Maybe selling well.

The third: he thinks he can get a date with someone from his marketing class, who conveniently has just joined the YMCA.

The fourth:

Kenneth stops by to pick up his negatives. He's happy because the photos of Gary in his portfolio got him hired this month for a well-paying shoot. Gary's pleased too. He and Kenneth are becoming friends, and a friend is a good thing to have. Also, come to think of it, he can't remember the last time he had a straight male friend, his social circle is mostly girlfriends and other gay men. It will be good for him.

They're drinking beer.

Kenneth excuses himself and grabs a package from the hallway, wrapped in angels and Christmas bells, a lop-sided silver bow in one corner. "I thought you should have this." Hands it over.

It's the calendar of Asian men. Gary grins at it. What else can he do? Except thank Kenneth sincerely, and give him a bear hug. He sees the calendar from this year just past above his kitchen table. Takes it down. Puts this one up. To welcome the new year.

The Polish Titanic

Due to outdated information in my *Let's Go* guidebook, my own unmistakable sense of timing, and a lack of command of the Polish language, I am running towards a huge ferry, lit up in the distance, and I am imagining it pulling away from me. I am huffing and puffing and sweating, my knees buckle as I push through the doors of the terminal. "Last one," says a uniformed official. "Passport please."

So I'll leave Poland. What a relief. This ferry from Gdansk is the only one until Wednesday and five more days of these February greys, the sooty blackened Communist architecture, the heavy dark winter jackets draped over slumped shoulders: all of it too much for me to take. Gdansk was pretty enough, a nice reprieve, but I'm anxious to get on my way. My six-month backpacking adventure in Europe is nearly half over.

Once on the ferry, exhausted and sticky with perspiration, I see only posters for Helsinki. I command myself to be calm. "Excuse me," I ask an attendant. "This goes to Stockholm before Helsinki, right?" She looks at me with dazed eyes: "No." My heart falls out of my body. What am I going to do in Finland? She translates the question to the attendant next to her and turns towards me again: "Yes, Oxelsund first, which is near Stockholm, then Helsinki."

Phew! No problem. The ship's motors rumble to a start and we move into the channel. The boat starts to rock. I make my way upstairs to the cafeteria where Italian disco thumps and other cabinless passengers stake out places in a section in the corner with round couches. The sea is certainly rough today. The floor is moving too much so I look up to fix my eyes on something else, just in time to see a man lean over and spew onto the carpet.

I rush to the washroom, marked WC: Water will help, I reason. Vomit is everywhere though, in the sinks, in the urinals, both of the unoccupied toilets. I flush one of them first before I fill it up again with my hot dog supper and other unidentified foodstuffs. I'm surprised at how much better I feel.

That night I sleep fitfully, moving from couch to cushions to floor. From the cafeteria with its non-stop Eurodisco playing over the intercom to a quieter spot downstairs where the red colour of the carpets invades my dreams, which are filled with running and shortness of breath and nausea. The air conditioning is at full blast in the morning, so I return to the cafeteria, still swaying in the rough waves.

~

The next morning I meet Piotr. I take the beat-up old guitar I travel with to a quiet corner on the landing above the slot machines. It is my security blanket, my fellow voyager, and as the boat continues its wild dance, I spread my legs far apart for stability and begin to play. Piotr approaches, shyly, in stages: first, standing at the bottom of the stairs looking up, then part-way up the stairs until finally he stands against the opposite wall listening as I croon my best Tracy Chapman.

"Do you speak English?"

"No, no. Little."

I beckon him to sit down, point to myself. "Andy."

"Piotr."

We shake hands.

"Beautiful." We talk as I strum.

"Stockholm?" He nods. His eyes gaze up into a pocket of air. He reaches into it and pulls out a word. "Uncle."

I grab my datebook, draw him a rough map of Canada, lines shaky under the rocking of the boat. When will these waves stop? I place a black dot on the south-west corner to show Vancouver. He takes his turn, drawing Poland to show a small town south of Gdansk. We exchange ages. He is one year older than me.

He wants to tell me something. "You," he pauses, looks up to grab a new word. "Guitar. Big music," he motions. "Me." He stops.

"Do you want me to teach you something?" I query with appropriate hand motions. "Or play something?"

"No," he shakes his head vigorously "I . . . don't know." He breathes out in defeat.

"Maybe someone else can help? Someone who speaks Polish and English." I put my hand over my eyes in a searching motion. "Excuse me," I call out to a young couple passing by.

"Sure, we speak English," they say.

"OK!" I motion to Piotr to ask them something in Polish.

"We're Finnish!" they respond and walk away.

Confounded, I play another song, to which his eyes light up. He motions a beat, sticks, rhythm: "Drums," I exclaim, "you play drums."

"Yes," he smiles. "*Collegas* . . . mm."

"Oh, you played in a band with friends, with *collegas*."

He gives an unsure nod, "Yes," then "I . . . don't know."

I look at him, strain to understand this unfinished sonata woven of intuition and effort. Like talking with infants or the very old, I go by different clues than words alone.

"I understand you," I nod, and he nods too, tentatively.

Piotr is about my height, not too tall and not too short. He has the broad squarish face of some of the Poles I have seen, medium short wavy brown hair, a light moustache hovering above a wide mouth, and skin the colour of tea with too much milk, creamy but not pale, like a Greek statue. He's handsome, in a boyish, friendly sort of way.

When the announcement comes over the loudspeaker, I see his eyes roll up, his face falls into a silent groan. 'Ah, it can't be that bad,' I think.

> *– Attention, please, attention! Due to the weather and technical problems, we will now be heading back to the port of Gdansk. Further instructions will be given upon arrival. Thank you –*

My eyes roll up, my face deflates. How long have we been gone? Another announcement comes, in three languages. Finally, in English: *– passengers are invited to a complimentary breakfast in the dining lounge. –* "No pay?" I say to Piotr. "*Gratis*," he replies. Fourteen hours into a twelve-hour ferry ride and we're rewarded with free food. The thought of a full buffet table makes me gag. I imagine it being eaten and then thrown up as if the ferry is a bovine second stomach.

In mutual despair, we head back to the cafeteria, but the boat gains a second wind, lurches and rocks with even more force. The sound of glass breaking: bottles and drink containers collide with each other. I wedge my guitar into a safe spot and we head downstairs to explore. I stop a ship attendant on the way down. "We'll be in Gdansk by noon," he tells me.

The lobby is chaos. The ship lists heavily to one side. Suddenly a table careens across the floor, then chairs, and more. Elderly women grab onto each other's chairs to stay in one place, children are crying, a stroller trundles across to the other side of the ship. I struggle to keep my balance, legs wide apart, and notice two women sitting on the stairs, each of them one hand wrapped around the rail, the other held upturned in front of their hearts, a rosary and cross in their palms. One cries and the other prays.

My mind also turns to spiritual matters. Why am I here? What will happen to us? What if I die? I swallow my fear, laugh nervously at the commotion and get to work, speechless as the ship leans to the other side and the objects and people slide back. Piotr is helping a group of women in chairs, I lurch to retrieve the stroller. The child wails in the corner. The room is tense, waiting for the next tilt. Headlines flash before my eyes: POLISH TITANIC! – *Baltic storm claims passengers – Lost at sea*. Piotr catches my eye and we nod, each seeming to understand what the other is thinking. I return the stroller, nod to an old woman, sitting in a low chair, steel arms wrapped around the only post in this section. She yells over to the mother of the crying child. I understand what's happening. They should be moved to a safer place. Where's the crew when you need them?

I grab the hand of a small boy, tears streaming down his face. Piotr grabs the stroller, the mother takes the calmer older daughter. We shepherd them down to the cabin belonging to the older woman and leave them there. Piotr and I look at each other again and breathe a sigh of relief. We've done our good deed for the day. He seems like an old friend.

We stop in front of a map on the way out to the lobby. He points out his hometown on a real map, then, the place where he did his military service. We hear another announcement, one that Piotr rolls his eyes at but seems to have heard before. He explains that the wind is coming directly from Gdansk, so although the ship came south, we have been blown past Gdansk. He points towards the east. The point just above Gdansk is where we keep blowing past, the port of Hell, or that's how it sounds in English. "Hell?" I ask incredulously. "Really? It's called Hell?"

"Yes," he replies, understanding that something is funny but not knowing what it is. "So . . . ship . . . here . . . try again." He indicates that we are trying for the second time to reach Gdansk by heading north.

I laugh and point to the east of the map. "Maybe more easy if ship goes to Russia."

"Or . . ." he says, pretending to swim.

"Yeah." I look at my watch and show him. We left Gdansk twenty hours ago. "I can't believe it." He nods in agreement with the expression on my face.

We are invited for more free meals. I imagine the pantry

is empty by now. We eat with the two Finns I earlier mistook for Poles, both students, one of philosophy, one of chemistry. The philosophy student tells a joke: "Descartes goes up to a bartender who asks him, 'Would you like a beer?' To which Descartes replies, 'I think not.'" The Finn raises his eyebrows. "And then he disappeared." It takes me a second or two to understand; his girlfriend groans and hits him on the shoulder. I look to Piotr helplessly. This I can't translate.

I think that talking to someone who doesn't speak your language is both difficult and easy. Difficult if one side talks too fast or if both sides give up too quickly: one of these usually happens. But if it works, it's like dancing on the moon, you pretend you understood one thing in order to understand the next and suddenly you've understood the whole of it, more or less. Piotr and I may not know many words of each other's language, but we are communicating. However, now he's becoming quiet, and even if I try to include him in the conversation and direct questions his way, he seems to be understanding less.

When we finish dinner, a lifeless slab of meat and soggy potatoes, I grin, "*Gratis.*" Another free meal. Not only must we look at the bright side of life, I note, we must be getting into port soon, it's nearly nine o'clock, the lights of the city call in the distance. Another crackle of the intercom, another announcement. I expect instructions on arrival procedures. Maybe there will be free hotels. I wait for the English translation:

– Attention please! We regret to announce that the port of Gdansk is now closed for the evening and we are not allowed to enter the harbour. We will be anchoring here for tonight and arrive in Gdansk tomorrow morning at the earliest possible time. Thank you –

Open-mouthed, Piotr and I look at each other once more and sigh. An older man passes by and speaks in Polish to Piotr.

"What is it?" I ask.

He points down the corridor.

"Cabins?"

He smiles. "Maybe *gratis*."

Minutes later, he returns from the service counter, beaming, keys dangling from his finger. After grabbing our packs from upstairs, I follow him down the hallway, feeling a mixture of gratitude, self-righteousness, and excitement: how good it is to get a cabin, how much we deserve it. Piotr relaxes in his bed, I take a quick shower.

A knock on the door and in comes a thin man with a matching thin face, young, dressed in a blue suit, carrying a briefcase. He doesn't explain himself, asks if the bottom beds are taken, groans when we tell him they are. He briskly places his luggage on the floor and hangs his stylish coat on a hook.

"Are you from Poland?"

"Actually, I am living in Sweden and work there now,

but I speak English and Polish as well as Swedish." As if to prove this, he says a few quick words to Piotr who smiles and nods.

"Are you working on board the ship?" I ask.

"Oh no. But I have friends here. I'm working on many things. We'll discuss it later." He is out of the room as quickly as he came in.

Piotr decides to go to sleep. We talk as he slowly undresses. His skin is soft and smooth as he unbuttons his shirt, but keeps on a thin white undershirt.

"Your uncle," I say pointing to him. "He will wait . . . ferry terminal?" From what I understand, the terminal at Oxelsund is an hour or two away from Stockholm.

"I don't know. Maybe . . . sleep there. He will see news. Call mother, maybe."

He has a tiny cross on a chain around his neck. "Are you religious?" I ask. "Church?"

"No," he shakes his head.

"Me neither," I reply. "Girlfriend?"

He looks at me in surprise, as if to say, How could anyone not have a girlfriend? A thought flickers behind his eyes, "If mother . . ." he says, biting his arms in worry and panic, "then girlfriend . . ." And he acts out someone biting her whole body in worry and panic. We break into laughter.

He takes off his pants and folds them, laying them neatly next to his bed. He lifts the sheets up and slides underneath, a strong, athletic body. I imagine him playing sports, building things around his house.

"A normal life," I sigh quietly with a last look at his sleeping form. "My handsome new friend." Before I fall asleep, our other roommate slips back in, throws his briefcase on the bed. "Hey, why are you guys going to sleep so early? You should be up and dancing."

"We're tired," I mumble, annoyed.

"Hey, you don't mind if I come in here later, with some people, with about four or five girls, if there's no room in my bed, I can slip some of them into yours."

"Just don't make any noise," I say flatly, "and keep them all in your own bed."

"Hey, what do you think of Polish girls? Did you have a Polish girlfriend? Did you sleep with any Polish girls while you were here?" Suddenly inquisitive.

"No." I'm tired and I want to sleep.

"Why not?" he asks, persistently.

"Because I prefer men," I reply.

"Oh shit . . ." he hits his hand to his head, straightens up and laughs in disbelief.

"Well OK," he says, getting ready to go. "I'll bring you some guys, blue eyes or brown?"

"It doesn't matter." I place my head down with relief that he is finally leaving us alone.

~

It is nearing thirty-six hours now since our ferry left Gdansk. We have breakfast with a tall dark-haired Pole named Robert. We complain about the ship and we chit-chat. Robert translates almost everything he says into Polish so that both of us can understand. Now, instead of searching my face and voice for meaning when I say something, Piotr looks immediately to Robert for a translation. I ask Robert what Piotr was trying to tell me earlier when I was playing guitar. They speak in Polish. "He wanted to tell you that he played drums in a band with some friends a few years ago."

"Oh, I figured that out already," I reply with a nod to Piotr.

"I'm staying in a cabin with some other friends. Let's meet up again later," Robert says cheerily as he leaves our table.

We nod back. "We'll have lots more time for that, eh?"

Finally, after a day and a half on the high seas, we pull into Gdansk where we spend the morning waiting for another ship. Some passengers leave. There is a long queue of angry people at the service counter.

We see the rat-faced roommate. "My friends who work on the ship tell me it was the closest to an actual disaster that they've ever experienced. One of the windows was broken, there was water on the navigation equipment, and the ship was too old to really be out in that sort of weather." I shake my head in amazement.

Piotr and I breeze into town where he buys a pack of playing cards. We walk around and he unsuccessfully tries to call his mother. I call my friend in Stockholm, tell him I'll be coming in late. We go back to wait in the terminal where I teach Piotr how to play a card game called Spit. He's confused at first, but learns quickly and soon is as good as I am. We exchange addresses too, he gives me his home address in Poland as well as the address of his uncle in Stockholm. We see Robert again just as we're told the boat is almost ready. I ask whether he thinks there will be new crew. "Of course," he replies.

"That's too bad," I lament. "The old crew is somewhat responsible for the disaster and so must feel a sense of guilt and duty towards the passengers. We could get them to do almost anything! This new crew just won't be the same."

Robert giggles and translates for Piotr.

On the new boat, Robert introduces us to his roommates, Arthur and Kristof. We head over to the bar. New friends, Piotr treats us to a round of beer, waving his American money a moment too quickly, awkward, eager to please. We make a toast in the busy ship's "Country Bar" as music booms from a TV sitting on the counter hooked up to a video machine with a crudely recorded mix of music and videos.

Two short broad Finnish men are sitting at the bar, obviously weightlifters or something of the kind. I mime to Arthur and Kristof a gorilla scratching its armpits. They howl. The rat-faced young Pole, resplendent in suit and tie, saunters in and begins talking to the simians at the bar.

I point him out to Arthur. "That guy was in our cabin with us last night." Arthur raises his eyes in surprise. "He likes to talk."

"Oh," Arthur laughs, "I don't like him either. I met him when we first got on, we were talking Polish and he pretended to not understand us. *Italiano*? I asked, *français*, English? I thought he must speak Japanese or something, he shook his head to everything. Later, I heard him speaking Polish, I thought . . ." He leaves the sentence unfinished.

Kristof nods and adds, "I don't like this type of man. *Ksiaze*, eh? Arthur." He turns to me. "We have a special word in Poland for this type of guy but I don't think it translates."

"Big shot. Bullshitter?" I offer.

"No, no. It doesn't translate. It's someone who tries to be very important, dresses up like that and thinks he's more intelligent, better than everyone else. Like that," he indicates, as we watch the man swing his briefcase up onto a chair.

"He has a face like a rat!" I say and we all snigger before turning away and ignoring him, just as he is ignoring us.

Cheesy, bouncy, electric music booms out. I glance over to the TV screen. Huge, buxom, interchangeable naked women sway to the rhythm, first one, then another, then a group, absurdly standing in a tropical pool, plastic telephones in hand and held up to their ears. I watch their eyes widen: Robert with amazement and desire, I think; Piotr with curiosity but trying to look nonchalant. Arthur raises his eyes and looks away, he seems to have seen this before. Kristof smiles and laughs in unabashed amusement.

Arthur leans over, "You should have come dancing with us last night – we were with two beautiful Polish girls trying to decide who would get to dance with them. But finally, one of them grabbed Kristof here. They danced the whole evening."

"At the beginning of the evening," joins Robert, "they danced very respectably." He mimes a formal distance. "But as the night progressed, they got closer and closer." He guffaws "But they were both wearing their passports and money under their shirts so they couldn't get too close."

Kristof admits with a shrug, "We came close and she apologised for the money belt under her shirt. I said, 'I know, I can feel it! Can you feel mine?'"

We burst into laughter. The music video is almost finished. The bartender rewinds it and plays it again. A heavily made-up woman bartender dressed in tight white blouse and high heels walks by with a drink.

"Woohoo," says Kristof. "What do you think of that?" I raise my shoulders, a noncommittal shrug. "We're both married, Arthur and I."

Arthur adds, "It's just for fun, just talk, nothing more."

"Ah, if there's more, it's OK with me," winks Kristof and the video starts to play again, breasts bouncing on the screen. Someone yells at another patron to stop blocking his view. The waitress, the only woman in the room, walks by again.

I look at her, so womanly, so feminine. I decide to change the subject. "Tell me some Polish police jokes." Robert translates my request for Piotr. "I've heard it's a national sport." I tell them one I learned to get the ball rolling, then another, which Arthur already knows. So I get him to tell it in Polish to which we roar and slap the table as he imitates the policeman, miming a fish in a store window.

We're off. I tell them my waiter-with-the-thumb-in-the-soup joke. Robert tells, with less success, a few bar jokes. I finish with the complaining alligator joke, complete with actions and sound effects. There is minimal translation needed. It's a hit!

Piotr leans over to Robert across the table, Robert relays to me, "He says that he wouldn't understand half of what you're saying if you didn't use your body when you talk."

The video changes to a bad duet by Dolly Parton and Kenny Rogers and I wonder if the men that I sit with were not so interested in tropical soft-porn music videos when something else interesting was happening. Maybe they were just doing what was expected of them. Then again, maybe they would rather have watched the video but were too embarrassed to show it. I like to believe the first theory.

We get another free meal that night, more greasy french fries and meat ("*Gratis*," I repeat, smiling). We all eat together: Robert, Arthur, Kristof, Piotr and I as well as the two Polish women that had danced with Arthur and Kristof the night before, Alicia and Renata. We arrange to meet later that night to dance in the upper lounge. The men head over to the bar, and we begin to drink again. A little drunk, I decide to wander back to ask if there are any french fries left. I return, unsuccessful, and Arthur and Kristof tell the rest of us to go back to the cabin where they'll join us in a little while.

We all crowd into the room, Alicia and Renata soon join us too, broad smiles all around, animated conversation – a mix of Polish and English. Soon Kristof and Arthur show up with a huge platter of french fries, to my joyful surprise. "For our Canadian friend," they beam. They pull out a bottle of Polish rum and pass it around.

That evening we dance until late. We pool our money to buy a pitcher of vodka and orange juice, and watch Arthur and Alicia, and Kristof and Renata twirl around the dance floor. Robert explains, "It's Polish dance school, everyone knows how to do it in Poland, except for me . . . I could never figure it out." The two couples twist around, and glide effortlessly into each other and away, dancing ballroom to Italian disco. A song ends and Alicia comes and grabs Piotr as Arthur leaves the floor. "That's what I like," he says. "These two are not typical Polish women. I like it when they ask a man to dance and say what they want!"

Even I am dragged onto the floor where I do my best to keep time. I don't dare consider more difficult steps. We stay here, Kristof and Arthur flirting with the two women, all of us relaxing and drinking, now forty-eight hours into our voyage. In the back of my mind, I wonder if we would be sitting here together if they knew that I would rather flirt with Piotr than with either of the women here. All the camaraderie and laughter, the french fries and jokes, what would be left?

"I'm getting a bit tired," I announce. Piotr looks about the same. "Shall we go," I motion and he nods in assent. I haven't felt this sort of easy companionship for so long, the sort of agreement of schoolboys to pal around and be together. We leave them to dance longer, and Piotr and I go off to sleep in the chairs we've found for the night, no free cabins this time.

~

The morning sun makes it way through salt-sprayed windows. We gather our packs together and head down to the crowd in the lobby.

"Piotr," I say. "What is this in Polish?" I close my eyes and pretend I am sleeping, than I shake my head as if caught in a bad dream.

He thinks for a second. "*Zmora.*"

"Ah, *zmora*, nightmare," I point downwards at our feet. "*Pomerania, Silesia,*" I say the names of the two ferries we've been on. "*Zmora*!"

He grins.

"WC," I say and head off for a quick pit stop before we arrive.

When I return down the stairs, I look around for Piotr and see him with the Polish *ksiaze*, dressed in his suit and briefcase. My heart clutches, a flower's bloom in reverse. What are they talking about? This rat-faced man is my nemesis: it's his last chance to hurt me, a final annoyance – or more. I scan Piotr's face for clues: surprise, shock – it's hard to say. One time, he gives an expression of thought – puzzlement? A glance downwards and to the side as his mind shifts – the look passes from his face, a cloud rolling past the sun. It is gone as the *ksiaze* slips off into the crowd.

My mind whirls as I move towards Piotr, a few feet away, and wait with him in line to leave the ship. I'm defensive now and I know I could put interpretations onto the blankest spaces, where none belong. But still, he is so quiet. Self-consciously, I make jokes as we descend the stairs. "*Do widzenia Pomerania, Do widzenia Silesia*, Goodbye goodbye Polish ferries." I wave at the ferry, and invoke the names of our two Titanics one last time. A young woman looks over and laughs. "Goodbye Polish *zmora*, goodbye free food," I say as we push onto the crowded shuttle bus. Piotr smiles, is silent.

Off the bus and to customs we walk; he signals to me to look to where his *voi*, his uncle, is waving. Piotr waves back, wordless communication, 'I have arrived, see you around the side.' Voi Wojtek is an older man and looks very Polish in his winter hat with earflaps. He disappears for a moment. I imagine calling and meeting him, perhaps going to his place where Piotr and I could go out for a beer. I could meet his small cousin, Wojtek's son, maybe Wojtek could translate between us. His wife, I'm sure, doesn't speak very much Polish. Maybe I could find out a bit more about him, make a toast to this bright new friendship arising out of disaster.

We see our Polish friends again. The two women are waving at two tall handsome men standing where Piotr's uncle was standing. Kristof and Arthur look at each other, shrug and laugh. We all say goodbye and good luck, shake hands, kisses on cheeks. Wojtek reappears and is waiting patiently, we see him through the glass. "Everyone move back to behind the line," indicates the woman in the glass customs booth.

"Piotr." I reach into my back pocket and bring my hand back in front of me, as if I'm performing a magic trick. I've ripped the small cloth Canadian flag from my backpack. I press it into his hand. He looks surprised, pauses, reaches . . . then pulls out the pack of cards he bought. He hands them to me. "*Dziekuje*, thank you." He nods. Is he distant or not? Maybe it's my imagination.

He moves to the counter and I wait behind the white line. What an adventure, I think. What a disaster! Over sixty hours to make a twelve-hour journey. Piotr is approved, his papers are in order, he moves through the gate and past the swinging doors. There is no problem for me either. A customs officer looks carefully at my passport and smiles when I thank her in Swedish, "*Tusen Tack.*" I follow the corridor and scan the signs: green arrow for nothing to declare. I open the door to a waiting room crammed with people. I walk through it to a parking lot, cars, buses, more people.

Piotr didn't have anything to declare, his bag was smaller than mine. Still, I look back, expect him to come out of the crowd and beckon me towards his uncle's car. I walk jerkily, quick and slow, look back to the waiting room and out to the parking lot. The rat-faced man pulls out in a sports car driven by a tall woman. I do not look at him.

People load their cars, bundle children and luggage into empty space. A light wind carries the sharp edge of winter. I search much longer than necessary, guitar in hand, pack on shoulders. Maybe his uncle wanted to leave right away, maybe they were parked in the far lot . . . Somehow I don't believe it. The wind blows against my face like a hand dipped in the ocean waves.

Goodbye, Piotr, I think. Goodbye.

Travel

Reese plays guessing games on the phone. If he can't see the person he's talking to, he wants to make sure they're alive. So he raises the level of emotion in his voice, becomes a curious child, directs his energy into the telephone wire like lake water being channelled through a sluice to a different place.

This is why when Laurie says to him, I have news to tell you, the mouth shaping the word "news" so it is bright, meaning good news, the throat polishing the word shiny, meaning important news, he tries to guess what it is.

"Are you getting married?" he asks. No, that couldn't be it. Laurie may have admitted to really falling in love with Mitch, who she'd met on a development project in Guatemala. But marriage was something else.

"Well, pregnant? Nope. How about . . . Did you get the

contract for Peru? For the indigenous women's project?"

"No . . ." she pauses. "But you were close the first time. Why couldn't I be pregnant?"

"LAURIE!" Reese shouts into the phone and inhales his breath at the same time. "Really?!"

It was a surprise to them too, she explains, but it seems like a good time in their lives to have a kid. Everyone is happy. Mitch is excited. Both sides of the family are giddy with the news. "Hey, it looks like I'm going to be in Toronto for a while. What a change!"

~

It was a time when middle-class Canadian kids went off travelling. A year before university, a summer during, or maybe even a year between. The more adventurous sorts would head off to more and more remote places: Nepal, Chile, China. Europe was old hat, although one could get extra points (according to this particular scale) by visiting Eastern Europe, the less tourists, the better. Four points for Prague, eight for Sofia, ten for Tirane.

Still, Reese wanted to see the major stopping points. On his flight into Paris, he met Laurie across the aisle from him, the flight attendants punctuating their conversation as they scurried back and forth. Laurie was off to work for a cycling tour company, work she'd done before. "The groups of kids can be brats, but sometimes there's a nice group of older Americans. It's not bad work." She offered him a place on her floor for a few days, grinned with amusement at him, a guide to hostels tightly gripped in his hand, a Canadian flag peeking out from the small backpack tucked under the seat in front of him. He seemed barely able to sit still.

"Six months, huh? I'd say if you want to go through Poland, you should hit the Northern route. Amsterdam, Copenhagen, Berlin. Skip Brussels though, it's a bit sleepy."

Not precisely six months later, Reese gave her a full report. He was more wide-eyed than before, animated, nervous at returning home and tired of his limited wardrobe which was starting to smell of trains and hostels.

"Instead of becoming more known, it's like the more I saw, the more mysterious the world became," he told her, his face flushed with wonder. "It felt like something somewhere in my brain was growing like a balloon."

Laurie smiled and nodded and indulged his stories of avoiding other young travellers, being a bit of a loner and a snob, forgetting to eat while trying to save money, the missed train connections.

They made a giggly toast with red table wine at a sidewalk café. "To meeting again!"

~

They kept in touch. Reese turned into a traveller, his hometown smaller and the world larger at every new destination, pulled into a drawn-out undergraduate and then graduate degree. Laurie moved from Europe to Latin America, from tour guiding into development projects. They would meet when both in Toronto, and once even took a short holiday together to Mexico where they climbed the pyramid of the sun and lunched on avocados from the *mercado central.*

They trade admiration stories. Laurie says, how can you do all the things you do, travel, study and have a social life? Reese says, how can you manage to pack your bags on a minute's notice, not forget anything, and be organised enough to send all of us postcards?

There is something of each of them in the other. More in common than just a meeting in the sky.

~

"Greece! Laurie, how wonderful! Bring me back one of those plastic things filled with water and fake snow and the Parthenon or something."

"Snow in Athens? Reese, I'm not sure about that."

Laurie is a gift-giver. Reese figures if he requests something cheap and touristy, she won't go to too much trouble to get it. It amazes him, her lightness, her joy, her ability to make days celebratory. She takes an old friend out to a favourite boutique every spring to buy her a new outfit. Parties, dinners, housewarming gifts materialise. "Some days are special; other days, we make special." She winked at Reese when she said this, pulling a casserole out of the oven. Somehow it didn't seem corny.

The trip to Greece was another way to celebrate. She and Mitch would head off for a three-week holiday; they would spend time alone together. It would be perhaps the last time for a while that they could do this since trips would soon be baby-in-tow. "No Greek wine or ouzo for me this vacation," she stated with conviction. "Gotta start taking care of myself! Stop eating food on the run and partying late nights. Mothers need lots of rest!" Grinning, a sparkle in her dark eyes.

The broken white columns of temples and ruins scratched an azure blue sky. The sun turned their skin brown. In Canada, the lecturer is typically and disappointingly boring for someone with a fat tenure. Reese's mind drifts and he can picture Laurie, her long dark hair on her back, her stomach just starting to look bigger underneath an elegantly patterned cotton frock that would catch the wind as she walked. He always loved the way she dressed, even when they were travelling in Mexico together and they were tired and hadn't bathed, she would always look graceful and sharp in her travel wardrobe, complaining how awful she must look, although she never did. He tries to imagine what kind of maternity clothes she'll find.

~

"I'm so glad we're here, Mitch."

"It's sure a long way from Nova Scotia, isn't it?" Brushing back the light brown hair from his forehead, on the edge of a creaky bed, a shy smile, thinking of his hometown.

"I never thought our casual relationship would turn into this." She is fixing her hair. They are going out to a corner restaurant. "I worried about never settling down after all those short relationships. And now, I can't believe it. I'm feeling settled."

"On vacation? You're feeling settled on vacation?"

"You know, I think I am."

When they arrived back from Greece, the midwives' tests said that the baby was dying or dead. When she checked into the hospital, they said that the baby had died over a month ago, and that the only reason she had not miscarried was because her body was in such good condition. It had hung onto this small basket; she flew over the ocean and back and never knew.

~

Reese walks up the busy street to the house split into three apartments. Laurie and Mitch live on the second floor. The day is sunny like the pages of a holiday guide, but the wind is brisk and carries specks of moisture. It pushes insistently against metal doors of cars, branches newly weighted with summer green, Reese's hurried stride.

At the front of the narrow wedge of grass, in between the driveway and the walkway, sunlight hits the sleeping body of a cat. Reese turns to look at it, jealous of its leisure, and lets out a half-choked scream. The body is twisted unnaturally; the fur is bloody. He rushes up onto the porch and rings the bell to Laurie's apartment.

She looks wonderful, hair loose, her dress is a deep red, she wears a black smartly cut jacket over it. It is the first time he's seen her since she left for Greece. "All things considered," he offers, "you look great! Healthy and tanned. And is that a new dress?"

It is, one of few purchases in Greece since both she and Mitch are light travellers. "Let me show you my new shoes too." Their bedroom is bright and clean, simply decorated with a mirror and a few framed prints. They decide to go for a walk and then return for tea. "Is it cold?" she wonders. "I've been feeling so cold these days."

She had told him the news by phone. Few details. Just that they had been very sad. That both sets of parents had travelled to Toronto when they heard the news. That they wanted to try again. Soon. "It's been hard," she said, "but we're young, and I guess it's let me see what some other people have been through." Though he could not see her, Reese imagined her shrugging her shoulders, her lips pursing slightly as she caught her breath.

Laurie puts on her jacket. "Uh, Laurie, did you see that there's . . ." Reese motions to where the cat's body was lying.

"Oh," she lets out a tentative laugh at his embarrassment. "Yeah, it's been there since yesterday. Someone must have just left it there for us after running into it. What am I going to do?" she exclaims. "I wonder if there's a dead animal pick-up service in town. I hope I don't have to go around and knock on doors to see whose it is."

Reese lets out a sound of sympathy and horror. "Get Mitch to do it," he suggests. They cut across the driveway to the sidewalk so that they don't have to pass by the dead cat. She asks him questions about university, and what are his plans for the fall. He asks her all about the trip.

"We're turning into such chi-chi travellers," she says in mock horror. "Staying in a hotel instead of a grotty hostel." She describes cosy restaurants, the view from the hotel, the domed churches, the museums and their bleached amphoras and worn coins, the bus rides and reckless drivers.

And all the while, he cannot stop thinking about it. He looks up at the glint of the sun's rays on her dark sunglasses covering her eyes. Laurie, who he has always thought of as so strong, and here he is thinking that he should treat her as gingerly as a porcelain vase, the one in his living room in Vancouver, the oxblood vase, named for its rich red glaze that seemed to reflect and take in light all at once. It is from the T'sing Dynasty and is cracked. "A shame," his mother declared, "but accidents happen, and it was a good repair, you can hardly see the damage." Reese kept away from that vase, though its rounded wondrous shape was so tempting. He wanted to lean over the top and see whether the inside was as beautiful as the outside, although he knew it was too dark, and the neck too narrow.

Now he is walking on a street in Toronto and he is feeling guilty for treating her like that vase. Yet wondering if he should, and is that her voice cracking? He looks at her and sees his reflection in her sunglasses instead of her eyes.

"Well, I was almost glad we didn't know before the trip since we would surely have cancelled it right away, and we had such a wonderful time. Mitch and I get along so amazingly when we travel. You read these articles about couples who get divorced after travelling together, and I wonder how it could be like that. It's crazy, isn't it? To be with someone you can't travel with."

They pass a park filled with people tanning, parents with children, kids on swings, a man playing guitar on a bench, a woman jogging with small weights in her hands.

"At four and a half months, the baby is supposed to start to kick and yet I never felt anything," she tells him. "The midwife said it was because I'm so healthy, but still I worried. We're going to visit her this week, just to thank her for everything, and ask questions about my health and about our plans to try again."

The weather is warmer than when Reese first left his home this morning. They turn around and retrace their steps back to the apartment. When he first learned about the mysteries of a woman's body, Reese wondered if women understood death better than men, the wave of life that would fall and rise within them, half the world oblivious to all this internal motion.

"They say it's not unusual for women to have miscarriages the first time around. Of course, I have my own theories too. About it not being time yet, about the spirit not being ready to enter the world."

He nods, not quite believing it, but believing it, for her.

They arrive back at the apartment. Laurie jiggles the key in an ornery lock. In the kitchen, over herbal tea, it is time for the gift-giver to receive a gift. Reese had found it in his drawer, still wrapped. At the time he bought it, he was with his friend Sheila, who had told him that Toledo is famous for its jewellery of fine spun silver. He decided to buy a pair of earrings to tuck away for a special occasion. The woman in the store wrapped them in paper printed with a design of green knotted rope. He carried them with him from Spain and has held onto them for how long now?

He hesitates before he gives them to her. He's not sure what they look like now, they've been wrapped and hidden from sight for so long. They are perhaps too small, Laurie always buys long dangling earrings that match her flowing hair.

She unwraps the packet. The earrings are shaped like small silver moons dangling off of studs made of the same lacy silver fashioned to resemble tiny flowers. She grins, surprised. "What's the occasion?"

"No occasion," he replies. He doesn't bother to explain where they are from. It doesn't matter. He knows that she understands the value of gifts, how we travel far and wide for them and offer them with nervous fluttery hearts. How sometimes they are lost or broken or damaged in transit. How sometimes they survive.

Outside, the cat is still there. Who did it belong to? Have they noticed it missing? He forces himself to look at it as he walks by. The fur is soft and inviting where it is unspoilt. He has a sudden urge to turn it over with his hands. But the jaw is full of blood, eyes half open. A limb is sprawled awkwardly in a position that cannot be natural, even for cats. Its torso is leaning up slightly towards the sky, only part of the stomach showing. As if it could roll over and disappear into the grass.

But that is what he wants it to do. It may be organic material, fur and bones, a complex cluster of immobile cells, but it would take many years and many rains for the corpse to seep into the ground, the bits of fur to fly away in the wind, and the neighbourhood gulls to carry the bones into the sky, one at a time, like the steps of a ladder.

First, they prepared the eggs. Dai Mo, great-auntie, the one who chose my Chinese name, reached for the carton, her hands turned into a careful claw. She plucked out three oval shapes and placed them in the small pot filled with water. They added the dye, bought from a herb store in Chinatown, and lit the gas stove. The white shell slowly turned pink, then red, the insides hardened. Dai Mo hit the eggs with the spoon so the shell would crack and the red colour would transform the insides as well.

And then they were ready.

I only found this out years later. Mother and I in our basement, she was opening up the big black safe, the kind that belongs on movie sets. I have no idea where my father got it. She was storing away part of her small collection of jade carvings. Her hand exiting the safe paused at one of the shelves, reached into a shallow cardboard box and pulled out an envelope. It was marked with my name and a date: August 7, 1969. "This is a piece of your hair from your first haircut," she explained. We open the envelope gingerly, I don't dare breathe upon it. Inside, at the bottom of the envelope is a small clump of black down. "You had so much hair when you were born!"

Dai Mo cracked open the eggs and left the shells on a cloth on the kitchen table. Then she rubbed one of the rubbery hard-boiled eggs all over my small, soft head. "Why on Earth did she do that?" I asked.

"Well, it was to get you used to the feeling of something on your head – scissors, hands – it was for your first haircut, it was so you wouldn't cry."

"Well, did I?"

"I don't remember *that*," said my mother, and I saw her twenty years younger, not so different really: a more youthful face, blacker hair, the same calm pleased look as today, the older relatives all hovering over her, and over me too – grandfather, days before his death, Dai Mo's husband, probably drunk on Scotch like always, some of my father's brothers or sisters. Her youngest son, his first haircut.

~

I have always had mixed feelings about my name. Things could have been worse. Chinese daughters often get the names of flowers: Peony, Pansy, Jasmine. The sons get names of odd British men plucked from history: Winston, Byron, Percival. Growing up I had a theory about this. However antiquated these names might sound to Anglo-Canadians, Chinese families had no mental associations with them at all. They were simply names, one basically as good as another, so why not have something a little more flashy and important sounding than John, they thought, eyes lighting up with ambition.

I suppose that is how I got the name Samson, which I tried to hide under the moniker Sam, but which failed whenever a teacher at school would read out a roll call at the start of the year. The biblical reference was not so bad, as most kids didn't know who Samson was anyways, but once it started, it stayed, and from time to time, my classmates in the schoolyard would tease, Samson, oh Samson, where is your long hair? At least it was better than the kids that called me Samsonite, after the luggage company, the name with a faint Japanese ring and sounding like Superman's deadly poison.

People tell me I look different according to each of my haircuts. If I have it short, I look boyish; if it is long, I look older. It looks very different in a ponytail from when it is loose. Just as I believed others were marked for certain paths, I also felt that my destiny was linked to my hair due to my name and my biblical namesake. While I surmised that Myrons would always be awkward, that Jeffs would always be friendly, that Louises would tend towards cigarette-smoking, I knew that I, Samson, and my strength would always be linked to the long strands of straight Chinese hair springing out of my scalp and downward with gravity.

~

I went through many phases with my hair.

The first was the barbershop, the Greek barbershop that my father and brothers went to. It smelled of talcum powder and blue after-shave. There were mirrors behind the barber chairs and in front. When I sat down in the worn vinyl, I could see my head multiplied a million times, the smallest one receding off into the distance, somewhere too far away to see the end. I figured someday I would visit that place.

There were four barbers. Leo would nick my ears, Christos seemed so sloppy. Dominic was OK but it was his cousin Con who I liked, his large hands cupped around my head, the warm buzz of the razor against my neck, the blades of his agile scissors hovering around my scalp like the wings of a hummingbird. He would always give me the same haircut, just above the eyebrows, a bit above the ears. He would ask me each time how long I wanted my sideburns. He would shave the nape of my neck up to a precise horizon that curved around just below my ears.

It was when I was a tender fourteen that my outrageous friend, Luis, told me about model nights at Hiro's hair salon. Luis was outrageous because he wore stylish Italian clothes that were bought during summer visits to his grandmother's home in Rome, he wore a Speedo bathing suit for swimming instead of baggy athletic shorts like the rest of the boys, and he couldn't care less about the Rolling Stones and Led Zeppelin, the idols of the neighbourhood kids. He liked English bands with black dyed spiky hair. Of course, he would know about these special nights at the hair salon. Call them up, he advised. I decided it was time to leave the Greek barbers.

I went in for my first appointment. A young hair stylist named Chachka greeted me and led me to the back of the studio, all angles and black plastic and track lighting. The mirrors here did not reflect each other but instead other parts of the stylish interior. I was placed in a chair, my head placed back into a sink, caressed with sweet-smelling shampoo, massaged by strong lean fingers, my hair rinsed by a glorious spray of hot, hot water.

Chachka spent an hour on my hair, trimming single hairs here and there, consulting with her supervisor, clipping and unclipping metal clips used to divide my hair into sections. Instead of the crude equal lengths of the fluorescent barbershop, here at Hiro's they measured and primped, angled and gelled. She left my hair a bit long on top, incrementally angled upwards on the sides from short to longer. She trimmed off all remnants of sideburns and showed me how to gel my hair after she'd given me a second glorious shampoo. She blow-dried it all into place, and told me to come back in a few weeks. All for five bucks.

I returned many times. It was those days that I first

became conscious of how I appeared to others: I started to spend longer in front of the mirror, squint my eyes to see how I might look differently. I didn't like my face. The eyes were fine, a simple almond shape, like Mom's. I had heard of Chinese who had gotten an operation to have their eyes "fixed" so they would appear more Western. A slit here, a tuck there, voila! Eyelids. But I didn't mind that mine were hidden. The nose and the jaw were another thing. The former was flat and tended to sprout pimples right in the middle. I would have liked something smaller at the time, a bit more angular and delicate. As for the shape of my face, I couldn't stand its roundness. No one I had ever met who was considered handsome had a round face like mine. They had Superman jaws, angular V's or squared U's. Not my round ricebowl face. If I couldn't change my face, at least I could do something with my hair, which luckily for me, grew quickly.

I went through several variations of the gelled hairstyles that were popular in those years. I received them from a series of young, stylish, ambitious men and women who were at various stages in their salon careers. I made idle chit-chat, asked how long they had worked there, what they did before the salon, what kind of hair they liked to cut best. One of the stylists, a rough-looking fellow Chinese named Alexander, asked me about high school and studies. Just as he was finishing a final blow-dry, he asked if I had a girlfriend. Or girlfriends? It was not something I had really thought about, although I knew what answer was expected. Still, I was never good at lying. "No," I mumbled and, when pressed, said something about being shy. "Shy?!" he exclaimed. "C'mon man, you can't be shy about these things." He continued his pep talk as I placed a blue five-dollar bill in his hand and moved towards the door. I didn't return to him.

One of the next stylists, talking with his hands the way many of them did, described a wave in the air and said, "Your hair's getting long enough. You know what I'd do? I'd put a wave in it." I was starting to feel at the time that all Chinese hair was the same, and no matter what I did, I would look like all the other Chinese kids I knew. So I imagined that shape on top of my head, my hair sweeping over to one side, an ocean curve. It seemed daring and original.

Of course, that is not what happened, and I should have stopped it all when the rollers went in. "Samson! What did you do?" Mother asked in mock horror, although I could tell she thought it was quite funny: short at the sides but the rest of my straight Chinese hair bound up into curls on top of my head. Have you seen Chinese people with perms? I hoped people wouldn't think I was trying to hide my cultural roots. How embarrassing! My only consolation was that it was summer holidays and no one from school would see me. Also, it was easy to take care of. Pat it into place each morning; no need even for a comb. It was, however, a long summer and I decided then that I would grow my hair long.

~

Long hair! Long black hair! Silky, shiny, thick. The girls flock to it, they feel it, they braid it. "I wish I had hair like this," they exclaim. I reply, "I think you might look a bit odd with Chinese hair." Still, they giggle and flirt. I am different from the other boys. They are attracted to how little I care about the masculine requirement for short hair. However, they cannot seem to guess that I care nothing at all for masculine requirements.

That's not entirely true. The masculine requirement that I truly discard is that I should be interested in these girls who are interested in me. On other fronts I do want to be masculine. Or at least appear masculine rather than effeminate, which is what I've heard gay men are supposed to be. It scares me, this idea, not only that I am supposed to act a certain way but that I might be identifiable and subject to taunts or worse.

I manage to avoid accusations though, and it takes me some time to understand that as an Asian male, I am viewed as neither masculine nor feminine, or so I believe and so I carry myself. This allows me to meet those flirtatious looks with a completely blank stare that looks like innocence rather than distaste. Rapunzel, Rapunzel, I wonder, how did you know who you wanted to let your hair down for? Was it really love that climbed up those locks?

I grew my hair long the same time I left for college. While my mother thought my perm had been vaguely amusing, she was horrified by the increasing length of my hair. "Shouldn't you get a haircut?" she asked whenever I would appear home for weekend visits. The repetition would echo in my ears and off the walls, and I knew to expect it twice, three, four times a visit. There was no irony or playfulness in her voice when she asked the question. She simply hated that I had long hair.

It was about the same time that I was considering coming out, and somehow I managed to link the two issues firmly together in my mind. If mother couldn't accept my long hair, after my repeated moans and groans to stop asking me to cut it, how would she ever accept it if I told her I was gay? I kept my mouth shut. I kept my hair long.

When the girls would braid my hair, I felt the strands twist around each other, and I felt them twisting around me tightly and in all sorts of ways.

~

I have forgotten the dates when adolescence arrived. I only remember images. The hair that sprouted above my penis, all twisty like the shrubbery that grows next to the ocean, the curves and bends eluding the sea wind, rooting itself in place. I think I tried not to look those days, I much preferred to be smooth and hairless. I thought of my dentist's hairy hands reaching into my mouth, the tufts of chest hair rising above his unbuttoned collar. I felt nauseous.

I was lucky though, since I never grew much hair, hardly

any on my arms, a bit on my legs. As for other places, I watched my father cut his nose hairs and hoped I would never have to do the same. Eventually I would, that familiar revelation that we all become our parents one day.

I entered university. I told my parents I was gay, my father was confused and my mother cried, but she stopped complaining about my long hair. Within the year, things were relatively back to normal.

My mother started dyeing her grey hairs black. (I hoped that my sexuality and her grey hairs were not linked.) As for me, I discovered my first grey hair while on a drive in the countryside one sunny fall with a boyfriend, Paul, who was sweet but who would only last three weeks. "I can't believe it, I think I have a grey hair," I exclaimed in panic, holding it up and peering into the side- and rear-view mirrors.

"Where, where?" asked Paul as he lazily reached over while keeping one hand on the wheel. He found the hair and plucked it out with a sharp quick motion and a smirk. "Not anymore," he said.

Although I was annoyed, it was an easy solution at the time to the problems of aging.

I got crabs from the boyfriend after Paul. While I didn't particularly mind a bit of physical infidelity here and there (mental infidelity was another matter), I was dismayed at the physical consequences it had on me. I was going through an especially busy time at university and had started swimming again. I convinced myself that the itch was due to the chlorine. I almost fainted when I actually saw what was crawling around. Not only at being forced to face what my body had been telling me but also at these small horror-movie creatures with their white legs and prehistoric-looking forms. I considered shaving off my pubic hair, but realised that a simple powder was an easier solution.

After swimming I took up weights. Not only did I get to ogle beautiful men, but it also gave me a good topic of conversation, since it seemed that every gay man I met was going to the gym as well. It also appealed to my sense of vanity, and after believing my slight Asian body could not gain weight, I was quite pleased with the results.

I was amused with another discovery that summer. After admiring innumerable sets of perky, rounded pectoral muscles, some of which would lead down to an incredibly ridged abdomen, some of which would perch on top of a rounded or smooth torso, I started to wonder why they looked all the same, as if put through an assembly line to make parts of cars: hubcaps perhaps, or fenders.

I called my best consultant in the city, Randolph. Although he knew all the latest fads in the gay world, he never got too caught up in them. "Randolph, I've been noticing a disturbing trend lately. Why do all the men in this city have the same chests?"

"Ah," he put on his academic voice, which became more precise daily as he worked on his doctorate in social anthropology. "Perhaps my dear Samson, it is because not only are men body-obsessed these days, but they are all *shaving* their chests to appear even more masculine and true to form."

"But I thought hair was masculine."

"No, no. Where have you been, my boy? Gay men are dying into a sea of hair and ashes. Now, they all want to appear boyish and hygienic and hairless. The boy next door. It seems more healthy that way. Have you been frolicking with the gym Nazis lately?"

Hair. No hair. Shaved hair. Shaved chests. I thought about all of this with some satisfaction and some resentment. Resentment since I could never fit into these gay North American obsessions. I may be a Chinese neighbour, but I would never be a boy next door. At the same time, I felt some sort of secret satisfaction. My chest was smooth, I would never have to shave it, I would never have razor cuts over my heart. At least, in a technical sense, according to the whims and styles of the gay community, I was one step ahead without having to do anything at all.

~

I travelled the country and other continents with my mane of black hair. I revelled in the attention it brought me. Sometimes, I would be angry that it was all people could see. Many times I was addressed as "miss" or "madam" and would answer in my deepest, most resonant voice. Watch them try to hide their embarrassment and surprise.

While some white male friends with long hair would tell the same story of people approaching them from behind mistaking their gender, I don't think they'd ever been met directly face to face and addressed as a woman.

Where have these people been? I thought. Have they never seen a Chinese face? Can they not tell the difference between my slanted eyes and Suzie Wong's? Is my Adam's apple shrunken like our cocks are supposed to be? Are the breasts of Asian women so flat that they look like a thin man's chest?

Or do people not look? Do they see only a flash of black hair? A flash of something strange and foreign and unlikable so they turn their heads, so they speak with the first word that arrives to their tongues, so they stand, as in Columbus's supposed encounter with the indigenous peoples on this continent, awed by each other's strange tones of skin and manner of movement?

At the same time, I enjoyed hiding behind that hair. I could twist it when I was bored, I could cover my eyes with it when I did not want to see. I could hide my ethnicity in mystery. It was the Chinese who arrived in Canada in great numbers, my grandparents who owned produce stores and bought property, who raised children who moved step by step further into society. Yet still they did not understand us, or they believed that they understood us too well. The same questions over and over: What do you eat at home? Do you speak Chinese? Were you born here?

With long hair I could be almost anything. Few Chinese

had long hair. People would ask me if I was Japanese, Filipino, Thai. They would ask too if I was Indian, a native Indian, they would not know what word to use to least offend: indigenous, First Nations person, Indian? I could spin stories like thread, or I could tell them the truth, which was a long threadlike story since mother and father came from different generations of immigrations as well as different countries, even though all of our ancestors came from villages in the same province of Canton. If I wanted, I could be the ultimate Chinese. I was growing my hair, braiding it into a queue, to return to my roots, to wear my hair as the first Chinese immigrants to Canada did, if they managed to escape the white man's scissors.

~

There was another trend in the gay community that took me a while to notice. Randolph, of course, noticed right away, but knowing some of the background to my long mane of hair and secretly liking its connection with my name, he kept his mouth shut. The trend followed the same reasoning as the shaved chest phenomenon. If a hairless body, at this point in our history, was somehow more masculine and hygienic, what about hairless heads?

Gay men were shaving their skulls, their pates peeking out into daylight. Some had blue veins, some had razor cuts, others had odd bumps and lumps. If they were not shiny bald, then at least, hair was short. Short short, like crew cuts, a military allusion. Or short everywhere except for a cowlick that would rise up from the brow, like the Belgian comic book character Tintin.

I began thinking seriously about this trend. After all, it had been four years since I had seen my hair short, and I was admittedly tired of the long black hairs that would appear everwhere, thick Asian strands in the carpet, in the sink, in the shower and on bathroom tiles. I wasn't tired of the attention, but I was tired that it only came from women. There was, I must recount, a crudely drawn poster outside Toronto's Glad Day Bookstore that advertised a club for long-haired gay men and men who loved them. But to me, this seemed no different from the specialty classified ads that appeared in the back of the community biweekly seeking boot-licking slaves or water sport fanatics. To the mainstream gay man, I was definitely out of fashion.

Still, it was not an easy decision to cut my hair. When I told friends, most lamented what a shame it would be to lose such hair. Perhaps something clicked when I spoke with Terry, an actor friend of a friend. People always told me how intelligent he was but I had never seen this. He seemed to express only mild interest in me, and we only made idle chit-chat when we met. Besides, I was envious. I was deeply attracted to his physical form, a blond boy-next-door with a handsome rugged face, a football player's physique – a body that somehow avoided looking too planned and precise, unlike those of so many others on the gay scene.

"Don't listen to that crap," he said, his eyes elsewhere in the bar, sneaking a look at who his ex-boyfriend was talking to. "Why would you follow some stupid trend? Why would you need to follow the crowd? Gay people can be so superficial." His gaze shifted to watch a tall brunet cross the floor. "That's not a comment on you, it's just – why would you need to?"

I adjusted my ponytail, my hair drawn back and held by a thin black elastic. It's a game, I thought to myself. Checkers, parcheesi, poker. I want to play, and how can I play if people won't even let me into the game? I got up to leave and felt a flash of anger. I swallowed it. Heat bounced uneasily against my interiors. Terry could wear whatever he wanted, the most out-of-style clothes, the most garish colours; he could grow his hair into a river of blond; he could keep his chest unshaven if it wasn't already: he would still be pursued as he probably had been pursued all his life, men buckling at the knees at first sight of him. And he would never know that he did not need to play the game because he was it. He *was* the game.

When I shaved my head, I felt glorious. It was a nice surprise to learn my parents had given me a strong, round skull. I sent my braid to a Chinese-Canadian artist friend who thought he could work it into his next piece, a pseudo-museum display on the cultural artifacts of a composite Chinese-Canadian family. I showered and felt the hot spray directly on my head. My hair did not need drying. The number of hairs in the carpet slowly diminished.

Most important, I walked along sunny Church Street and felt the weather on the very top of my body, and amazingly, like a miracle predicted but not believed in, heads swivelled, other eyes caught mine. There is no way to describe to someone with no experience of swimming in the ocean how the salt smell rises into your head to the heights of your senses, how every inch of what surrounds you feels alive and in motion, how the salt leaves its traces on your skin as you leave the water. Ever since I had come out of the closet, I had had long hair, and I had never known what it was like to be close-shaven. More accurately, I had never known what it was like to be recognisably gay, and to walk on a gay street on a hot summer day. With all that mess of hair, the denizens of my gay world saw only an exotic creature with foreign roots. They could not see my desire through the forest of hair, could not name me as one of them. For with my skin already a different colour, they needed another signal to call me their own. Shaving my head, I had learned to play the game I wanted to play.

How many of you have ever seen your head bald, seen the lines and veins and patterns of the skull, to see how nature has formed that skull without the adornment of hair? That summer I saw it, and it was a revelation. Its round form showed me the shape of the world in which I was learning to take part.

~

When I arrived in Europe to start my first real job, in the office of a human rights organisation in Brussels, my hair was fuzzy, thicker than the skin of a peach but not so thick that the white of my scalp was hidden from view. Still, it was starting to jut out from behind my ears, it was losing its clean and even look. I was far too busy packing my bags before I left to give myself a quick shave; now I realised that the shape of the plugs was different here than in Canada, and before I did anything, I would have to find an adaptor for my razor.

It took me a few more days to find an electrical shop and even then the man handed me a small white plug that to me did not look sturdy enough for anything. When I tried it out, my plug still wouldn't fit into it. "Oh, that's easy to fix," said my French co-worker, Jean-Pierre, as a pocket knife suddenly appeared in his hands and he deftly enlarged the holes.

That night I was to meet an American friend, Reed, also new to the city. He had come to work for the European branch of an American newspaper. We were ready to explore Belgian gay bars for the first time. He would meet me here at the apartment where I was staying, which belonged to a friend, Thomas, who was away for the weekend. I finished work early and decided after eating some paté on bread that I would shave my head, take a bath, and be ready for action.

I stripped off my clothes, plugged in the razor and knelt in the bathtub, a mirror in one hand and the razor in the other. As I pushed this warm buzzing creature in straight lines back from my forehead, it reminded me of the Greek barbershop of my childhood. I started from the centre of my head and moved off to the right, the razor traversing my scalp like a sailor across rounded oceans. I could tell something was wrong, but it all happened so quickly. A small voice told me that the razor was overheating and that I must shut it off, but another voice said "Just a few minutes more." As I considered what I'd look like half-shaven, the second voice won. I heard a tiny pop, everything went dark, and a sweet acrid burning smell arose from my razor.

A few seconds passed as my eyes adjusted to the darkness, before I realised that not only had I blown the electrical circuits, but that I knew no one in the city who could help me. I stumbled around the apartment by the glow of the street lamps outside. I found a candle and lit it. I found ELECTRICIANS in the phone book just in case. Then I found the fuse box in the kitchen. Much to my dismay, despite fifteen or twenty minutes of flipping the switches into different formations, the power did not come back on. I took a bath in the dark and worried and felt sorry for myself.

I finally found the courage to call Thomas at his parents' home in Britain. Luckily, he was home. "Oh, you've blown the circuits, have you? Well look, you have to go down to the night store below the apartment, and ask them to let you into the basement to look at the circuits there."

It all worked out in the end. I covered my head with a bandana, Reed and I had a good night on the town, and the next day I sheepishly removed the cloth from my head at a hair salon and asked the woman there to finish the job. She was more pleasant than the European boys here, who were shy and hard to approach. I was the only Asian in the bars that night, and to me it felt like I was moving backwards in time, to a place whose cultural homogeneity had not truly been broken. We learn our lessons in one place, only to begin anew in the next.

Still, I figured that shaved would be the form in which I would stay in Europe. I arrived in this world with a full head of hair. Perhaps now to amuse myself, I could turn into a bald child, my round smooth cranium glowing in the light of new days ahead. A retelling of my entry onto this harsh, strange planet. If only it wasn't so cold in the wintertime. If only it wasn't so cold.

On the Paris Metro

The ceilings of buildings are always so high in Europe! I look up at the tall ribbed arc of the Paris Nord train station, and even with the bustle of people all around, I feel space around me as if I am floating up into the stratosphere, a speck of dust inside a helium balloon.

En route from my new job in Brussels to a meeting of European colleagues in Sitges, near Barcelona, I have to change trains in Paris. I don't remember cities in my home country of Canada having so many train stations. Here in one of the great cities of Europe, the trains travel in and out like blood vessels to a swollen heart, the arteries of the body stretch out in complicated directions. I follow the sign to the Metro and then in the direction of the line that will take me to the Austerlitz train station.

I see him before he sees me. First, the top of his head,

slightly balding, the pale crown peaking above wavy brown hair. At the same time, I see his dark blue raincoat sweeping back sharply as he moves towards the train. He carries a large soft leather briefcase and a small bag in his other hand, which is heavier than it looks since his tensed arm reaches out to give it space away from his stride. His suit, also dark, over a simple white shirt and an elegant tie, purple with red tones, shimmery. All of this I absorb in a few seconds as I try to follow his sharp handsome profile towards a set of quivering doors, about to close.

But I have my own baggage: my own soft briefcase, an attempt to look professional for my first job out of university, the forest-green backpack, which gives me away, my youth, my reluctance to part with it. Do you know how some people keep the same suitcases all their lives? Hard-shelled, difficult to carry, but orderly at least, rectangular to arrange neatly folded clothes and organised toiletries. I guess you move from there to those with wheels.

I am, on the other hand, the type to own backpacks. In fact, I have different models: for short trips, for long trips, for camping, for cities. I roll up my clothes so that they're more compact. I don't bring nor even own clothes that I need to fold neatly. I am thinking of this as I stare at the man in the train. He entered the subway car by the middle door, I by the side, intending to move closer. But a group of other passengers blocks the way. They take both sides of the car and lean into the aisle to talk with each other. He sits down, I am left standing.

I glance over at him and he is even more handsome than I thought. Like a fashion model or a *mannequin* as they would say here: strong jaw line, high cheekbones, dark eyes set back in a face full of character. A perfectly ordinary nose that does not throw the rest of his features out of balance.

I have always been fascinated when I see someone like this. What is it like to be beautiful? Do people know they are beautiful? Some, for certain, become very vain, their mirrors gain speech like in fairytales, they calculate others' reactions to them and experiment with different behaviours. Others must be a little confused. They know that people act differently around them: some fawning, some jealous and self-conscious, others purposely uninterested.

I was standing in a gay Latin club one evening talking to a friend. He was dressed in the smallest imaginable items of clothing for someone who was not hired to put on a show. An older man passed by, his neck twisting like a duck's: he cooed from beneath a greying moustache, "You're very beautiful." He brushed his finger on imaginary flesh, inches away from the tight black shorts, the sleeveless lace-up shirt stretched over Jim's muscular torso, over his six-foot-four height.

He looked embarrassed, not confused, but something else. "It's what God gave me," he called after the man. I was a bit surprised by the religious reference in the middle of a gay disco I thought of as secular. But it made me wonder too. How does it feel to know that through historical accident you are judged by your face and torso rather than the size of your feet or what makes you laugh? You are blessed and marked by this fact.

I have seven stops before my destination. A family with young children gets on at the sixth; the group of friends gets off at the fifth. I move into an empty seat, where I sit sideways, my backpack leaning against the window, my legs partly crossed on the seat.

This man I guess to be North American. He could be French, the slightly dark, handsome features. But Europeans usually dress with a splash of colour, something to brighten so much concrete grey space. I think that with his navy blue suit he could be Canadian, though I myself am dressed more colourfully, trying to look European. I am comparing our dress and thinking how very different we appear, how little time I have ever spent with someone who dresses and looks like he does.

He looks over at me with his dark eyes. I look back. We hold each others' stare. One second, two, three. I force myself to look at him, instead of shy away, for I know why he is staring at me, as he knows why I am staring at him. Finally, the corners of his mouth incline upwards, just a millimetre, and his head bounces once, an imperceptible nod. I turn away, filled with excitement, look at the book of gay fiction I am reading, fiddle with my train ticket, look up, look down, all in slow motion so as to appear collected and confident. He stares out the window, at the advertisements, back towards me, away. Surely he must be getting off at the same stop as I am, with all of his bags. Maybe he will even be travelling in the same direction.

The first time I was in Europe, a friend of a friend hosted me in a grand apartment in the beautiful old centre of Stockholm. He had met my friend Eron in a train station in London. "How did you do that?" I wanted to know, mystified.

Nils was slightly confused by my naïveté, slightly bemused as well. "You just know," he explained. "You stare at strangers you like, and if they stare back, then you go up and talk to them."

"Just like that?"

"Well, sometimes you don't even talk."

"What?!"

"Museums. You know, museums are great places to meet people too."

Nils doesn't know this, but he was the start of my great education on how to be gay – not the self-acceptance part which I was already quite good at – but the *men* part. He was about forty, conscious of his age, with wispy, wheat-coloured hair, which might have been greying but it was hard to say. He was a doctor, a neurologist, in a state hospital. "Taxes, taxes," he complained. "In Scandinavia, you're taxed to death if you have a good job. I'd be a rich man in America." He had a large bulbous nose and big eyes, like a comic book character, not the hero but part of the supporting cast. Still, he was tall and broad, with solid arms and shoulders. When he walked shirtless through the apartment, I wondered what it would be like to be held by this older muscular body.

I thought about staring at men on the street, and I realised that I have never stared at anyone in the street. Perhaps because I was slight, perhaps because I was Asian usually in non-Asian environments, perhaps because of my friendly face, I was harassed in public. Often enough to be wary, to speed away from the beggars who would focus their attention on me like hawks, to sidestep groups of young toughs, to fix my stare ahead into open space so I wouldn't be asked to sign a petition for Iran, for money for cigarettes, so I'd avoid racist slurs. How could I notice if someone was looking at me with sexual interest, when all I ever did was run away? I would have to reconsider my habits.

I learned another lesson from Nils. He had a new boyfriend, Trevor, who he wanted to spend some time with, so they decided to send me out to the biggest dance club in Stockholm.

"What are you going to wear?" he asked. Since he'd kindly done my laundry upon my arrival, he knew my wardrobe exactly.

I considered the question. "My jeans. Probably the blue shirt with the patterns on it."

"Hmm." He paused in thought while Trevor looked on amused. "Too woman," he said. "Got a t-shirt?" We agreed on my white t-shirt. "Got a belt?" I pointed out the one I had bought at an outdoors store, some manufactured purple material. "I'll loan you one."

I went to slip into the t-shirt, strung Nils's thick black leather belt through the belt-loops of my jeans.

Both of them stood there and evaluated me. His boyfriend, though a decade or two younger than him, was nearly the same height and build. They looked at each other and nodded. Then both approached me, one on either side. To my bewilderment, each rolled up one of my shirt sleeves, exposing a thin round bicep. "Now walk!"

And so I did, giggling, thinking it was a joke.

"No, pretend you have something really big between your legs. Stick out your chest. Walk slowly."

I did it, but I was still giggling.

"Now, go!" They shoved me out the door.

Much to my surprise, horror and amusement, that evening, I got the most attention I'd ever had at a club. Maybe it was because I was a stranger, and they don't see many strangers. Maybe because they don't see many Asians either. But I think it was at least partly because I decided to try the walk. And I made sure my sleeves didn't fall down.

I was chased by an awkward tall man with long hair and devilish eyes; a Swede who called me Samurai causing me to take to my heels; a portly older gent, round and short like an elf. I was also whistled at by a trio of Italian businessmen who beckoned me to come over. They looked like my father's business associates. I had never in my life been whistled at.

I didn't meet anyone I really wanted to talk to that

evening, but I did learn something. Was it like the first time one of our primitive ancestors discovered his reflection in the water? When was the first time you looked in the mirror and really paid attention?

This stranger across from me in the Paris Metro. Did he notice the way I was dressed, the silver earring in my right earlobe, my head shaven to conform to the latest look in gay urban centres around the globe? Or was it just that I was looking at him when he looked at me? Or did he right away think I was handsome? Or did he just see the book in my lap?

I am looking nonchalant. If there weren't people blocking the way between us, I would consider moving closer, but all the seats around him are still occupied. Anyway, I expect him to get off at the next stop, which is my stop, Paris-Austerlitz.

When the Metro car slows, I am looking up at him, and we watch each other with a warm steady gaze. I get up, still looking at him, the doors open, and people start to file out. But instead of getting up, he smiles, an acknowledgement, a farewell. If my face reflects what I am thinking then I look wistful, a smile of resignation, a small question hovering in my expression as if I have swallowed it, and am holding it in my lungs.

I walk slowly towards the stairs, watching him as he watches me leaving. He holds the same smile on his face until I am about to descend the stairs. I stop on the second one down and wait for the Metro car to leave. He can see my shadow, I do not know if he can see my face, but his breaks out of the soft curved line of his upturned lips into a full smile, the kind that you cannot hold for longer than a second or two because it would look false.

But there is no more than a second or two before the Metro car speeds away with an efficient roar and the sound of turning metal. The stairs lay themselves in front of me, down into the earth, and beyond that: Barcelona, my new job. As I follow the arrows which will take me to my next destination, I think to myself that this is what has happened to me all of my life. Strangers' glances. The misstep. The failed opportunity.

But I am lying to myself because I am lost in a fantasy about making love with the handsome stranger who has now disappeared. In fact, opportunities lie around every corner. Perhaps before I did not know how to see them, how to grab them. Now, from the evidence of my beating heart, the memory of our eyes locking, I know I'm on my way.

Ears

They hear that it's freezing all over Europe, not just in Budapest. Besides, it seems to have helped them all: two days into the "First European Gay and Lesbian Business Convention" and already the attendees are pairing up: love against the cold, hot embraces warding off the winter. It's what conventions and conferences are for, meeting people, which is all part of business. That's how the men would excuse themselves, since they are the ones doing it. The lesbian attendees, a minority, are off in caucuses or raucous women-only room parties while the gay men play their games of exits and entrances.

The first thing that Philip notices is the ears, they stick out from his head like ruffled wings, rounded pink half moons. Ears like this, Philip looks at like extra sexual organs. Bart is tall as a door frame, boyish haircut and grin, and a typical Dutch voice that rumbles at the low tones like gravel in a rainstorm. Bart is familiar somehow, a combination of past lovers and adolescent friends that Philip desired but never told.

But now he's telling. "You have sexy ears, I have to tell you. Other parts too, but the ears . . ."

Bart laughs, looks another direction, embarrassed. He's hooked up with someone else already, a Czech publisher with limited English but a dashing smile. But together in the bar, Bart doesn't look particularly thrilled with his catch.

Your move, thinks Philip. Slips into the crowd.

Bart is an obvious target, a school teacher from Amsterdam, here at the conference to take notes for his boyfriend, a travel agent in San Francisco. Lately, Philip is falling for school teachers, handsome bachelors nurturing young hearts and minds into further levels of maturity. They seem to like what they do, and have some sort of general concern for people, a kindness. This makes Philip go all mushy.

Philip also falls for attached men, the ones with open relationships or some sort of "agreement" worked out with their long-term partners. He finds that they have an unshakeable sexual confidence. When they flirt, it doesn't matter what happens: they know they always have someone to go home to. Plus, Philip is afraid of relationships, gets nervous if he thinks things are looking serious. Married men catch him off guard since he figures he doesn't have to deal with the future.

~

Two days of flirting later, he is tracing the shape of Bart's eyelid with his tongue. They move slowly as if wading through water. Bart's hand slowly creeps under Philip's shirt to find bare skin. Philip reaches up to breathe into Bart's ear. Irresistible, this ear, a swirling seashell with promises of ocean and hidden places. The mouth leads down to the stomach, nostrils lead to the lungs. But the cavities of the ears, they go straight inside the head, don't they? A direct entrance to the mind, to how we think and feel? He gently places his tongue from the outside rim to the inside whorls and then suddenly thrusts into the centre, in and out, in time with the motion of his groin.

A sharp knock at the door. Their eyes meet, raised eyebrows. "Yes?"

"Bart?"

"Oh Milus, I'm in the bathroom."

"OK. See you downstairs in five minutes."

"Milus? I'm . . ."

But he's gone. They look at each other.

"It's up to you, Bart. I'm not trying to barge in. It's just that I like you and you seem open to it." Always trying to explain things.

"I like you too, but I don't know myself." He shrugs, not knowing.

They tuck in their clothes and straighten their hair.

~

New Year's Eve and Bart is still flirting. They've talked about meeting in Amsterdam and Philip figures that he'll leave Bart and Milus alone. Though he feels like an off-centre spinning top, a beach toy. Liking Bart more and more and him approaching all the time, easing into flirtatious banter. Philip likes the attention, and hasn't found anyone else he's interested in pursuing. He sighs. Wonders what he's doing at this conference on this New Year's Eve.

The entertainment is tawdry but colourful: an off-key local singer cooing to a bouncy taped accompaniment, a costume contest among the dozen or so who have bothered to dress. It's won by a local boy dressed in what looks like a giant red vulva. The obligatory countdown rings through the ballroom. Abba's "Happy New Year" pumps loud, and all circulate, kisses shy and forceful, friendly and carnal, a rainstorm of lips.

"Happy New Year, Bart." Philip reaches up and the kiss is gentle, moist, just lips, no tongue. Bart looks affectionate, slightly distant.

Ten minutes later, Philip is finishing the dregs of his sweet champagne, a local brand, he's sure of it. He looks up and Bart is swaying in time to the music, an unfamiliar boy in his arms, bright red shirt, short feathered hair.

The room of the party is appropriately cavernous, high Soviet ceilings, a balcony and stairs at one side, tables set up around the edges and a small stage near the centre. As

Philip approaches the stairs, a stocky Hungarian he's spotted before grabs his arm. His eyes sparkle with alcohol and cheer.

In a hidden spot on the balcony, music swirling around them from below, they kiss passionately. In between hot darkness, Philip's eyes open and scan the space around them. His partner stops and looks at his watch.

"Boyfriend. Downstairs. Must go." He smiles sweetly.

Philip lets out a short low laugh and looks him in the eye grinning. "OK. You go down first."

"Never forget me?"

"Yeah." Nods.

When Philip descends the stairs, Milus appears, the charming smile missing, a bit out of breath.

"Bart, where is he?" A simple question, not an accusation. It receives only a shrug and a sympathetic grimace.

"Sorry. Happy New Year." His lips graze the Czech's pink cheek.

~

The next morning, Philip is like a three-quarters circle, begging to be closed. Angry footsteps on his way to the room. He needs endings, resolutions, a sense of completion. Though he doesn't know what it is he'll do if it is Milus who opens the door, or the other one, and not Bart.

The knock, the who-is-it? A reply in what is hoped to be a neutral tone. Bart's response is cheery, excited. "I was sleeping." A wide grin. White t-shirt. Those damn ears. A noticeable bulge in his black briefs.

An imagined scene: *He pushes smiling Bart into the room, strips off his briefs, grabbing hips and kneeling on the rough carpet.* Instead, he lets himself be led to the sagging bed and lies down on the well-used covers. He looks up, a tall silhouette over him. The light reflecting off the ceiling and Bart's ears lit from behind, like a boy's first erection, glowing red and pink in the dark. Their lips meet gently. Philip frozen and passive. Bart stops.

"Your eyes are dreamy. What are you thinking?"

Philip stares up. He is surprised when people know him from his eyes.

The words come out haltingly, a boat trying to get past shoals. "You know, I'm just trying to enjoy the moment. But I feel a bit like a number – there's your boyfriend in San Francisco, Milus outside and even the Estonian boy you were dancing with." He knows the number but he counts to himself, since he doesn't know what else to say.

"Who?"

"You were kissing some guy on the dance floor."

"I didn't have sex with him."

"And then you disappeared and Milus was looking for you."

"Oh." Caught.

Four? thinks Philip. Are we irresistible to him, or he to us?

Does it matter? The confession has been given. Philip closes his eyes, reaches up to stroke Bart's back. They start.

But the routine is one of interruption and when Milus knocks loudly on the door, calling, waits and knocks again, it doesn't matter if he'll come back or not, even after they hush and don't answer the door.

Bart and Philip pull on their clothes on opposite sides of the bed.

"Come visit me in Amsterdam."

"Yeah." Nods.

~

It's a cordial farewell, made with other people present. Philip is flying out earlier so he is the one to leave Bart standing in the organisers' office in the hotel, strewn with papers and cigarette butts, smelling of enclosed places.

In Philip's mind, however, it's different: *a sunlit forest, sparse but green, a brook runs through it, not quite deep enough to swim. Large rocks, big enough to sprawl on and catch the sun. Philip comes upon a spot above the brook. Bart, dressed only in his briefs, squats on a rock, looks up smiling.*

Philip looks for a path down but pauses. The rocks, the incline, slippery moss: so many ways of falling.

"Come visit me." The friendly growl. Philip watches as Bart's ears grow larger and larger. Pink see-through fans, seashells, china plates, they grow large as cymbals, then timpani. He flaps once, twice more and disappears into the sky.

Immigration

They make the decision for me, but I agree. Off to Gold Mountain I go, to seek my fortune. What does this land hold for me, people starving and hungry, unrest all over the countryside? In any case, we are adventurers, messages come back to our province from all over the world, India, South America, Africa. I go to follow in their footsteps. It is 1905, province: Canton.

~

When I told my parents that I was gay, my mother rolled her eyes, and my father left the room. "How can you decide to take up that lifestyle?" she screamed. "It is dirty, it is not accepted." Her eyes were glazed over with shock.

"It's not exactly a lifestyle, ma. I can't help the way I

am." I had notes that I had memorised, I had thought so long about what I was going to say.

"You are saying that you were born that way. Are you saying that you are gay because of us?"

"Maybe it's a gene, ma. They've been doing a lot of scientific work lately that seems to imply that there's some sort of biological cause for homosexuality."

"So you're saying it's something that was in my genes," she rolls her eyes a second time. "You are not homosexual, Albert!"

She leaves the room, I hear a choked sob. But nothing she says can change me. I have already started this journey and there is no changing my course. Maybe it was planted in my genes somewhere in my family history that I would be a traveller, that I would leave my home.

~

The voyage took forty days and nights. Flesh pressed flesh against cloth made stiff with grains of ocean salt. Stench of the sick and dying. Ghosts of those who did not make the journey. Nothing is silent. The waves have their own curved rhythmic language; the boat has its low grumbles mixed with high sibilants and long breaths. Everywhere the unspoken thoughts of the passengers are released into the hold, this enclosed space where they churn and find language.

~

I turn sideways to move through the cluster of people at the doorway, disoriented because of so many people, so much energy around me. The dance floor and bar are crowded. The sound of glass and metal taps, sink and water: drowned out by the insistence of a music that is like a solid object in the air, everywhere, pulsing.

I have heard that this is where I will find my people – strange, since I know no one. When you visit a fairground, or go to a large department store, you are never told that all the people around you are connected to you beyond the roller-coaster screams, beyond a stroll through the shoe department. Told that there is something about these people that is shared with you.

I don't know them. They look so different from me. I hear some of these men are sick, are dying. I see stares that I don't understand. But the sea of people opens a little at the edge. I slide in and rise and fall with the motion of the waves. I close my eyes and swing my head sharply to one side and then the other, an arc of black motion. I lose myself. When I finally leave the space, I am joined. In the night air, hard of hearing, voices around me that I hear muffled. We read each others' lips and understand what is being said.

~

When I set foot on this land, I knew that the language would be foreign but did not know how quickly I would be thrust into it. They took my name from me right away, its square shape, horizontal and vertical strokes, long and short, and suddenly it was flattened down and stretched wide into unfamiliar curves and valleys.

Gwan was my family name, a dip in the voice as it is spoken, an honourable name, one of the four horsemen who saved China. In the language of the white ghosts, it was made Quan, a long flat tone, a hardening of the opening note.

I recognised that the tongues in this new country could not make the sounds of the old country, but at first I did not recognise my new name. Travel changes the cells in your body, in your mouth, ears, and throat. But when you can't travel back, it is your heart that changes.

~

At first, I was gay, maybe homosexual. Neither word felt right on my lips. The first attached itself to images in my head that scared me. The second was a species rather than a name. So I discarded the second, and worked at learning why I was scared of the first.

I learned to wear the name in many forms: a confession, a confidence, a statement, an assertion. And when a new name came along, I grabbed at that too. Queer sounded like Queen and Quan, my family name. It was spicier than gay, more attitude, wider and less defined. The mouth lingered on it longer. Perhaps I felt that changing names often would keep people on their toes, for I resented that time when people first knew I was gay, and my first name was replaced by labels. No longer was I Albert, or Albert Quan. I was gay first of all, homosexual, faggot to some. I waved the names like flags and then searched for my old ones again. But I could barely find them. I knew I'd never be that person again.

These days, in the universities, young men with square glasses, patterned facial hair, the new academics, talk about giving up names completely. Why name ourselves by attributes that history paid little attention to a century ago? Furthermore, they say that gays in Africa and Asia often have no name, they simply are. So why call them by foreign names at all?

I say: give us many names, one for each section of our skin, for each thought in our head during the day, for all of our particularities and for each trait we share. There may be people who would read a book with a blank cover, travel to countries without names, and knock on doors without markings, but I am not one of them. Maybe it was my upbringing that taught me to be careful.

~

Funny, but sometimes when I'm talking lately, I will lose a word. It appears in front of me with an image or a colour and then I can't find it, an empty space the size of a marble in the back of my mind. It's not as if I can speak the language of white ghosts very well. Enough to get by. Survival. But I get so weary if I have to speak for too long. Exhausted from listening with all my might to make sure I understand.

Then how could I lose my own language? There is light here that does not come from flame or coal. Electricity. A tiny filament that brightens so much you cannot see it and daylight pours out of a small glass bauble. How can I describe this in Chinese, something that doesn't exist in my village? Who gets to name it? The man who returns to his village after four and ten years? A travelling salesman from the city? A lost foreigner washed up on shore?

If I forget words, how will I teach them?

I had a dream that I was wearing an ornate costume with pieces of embroidered silk, tassels of knots with forty and ten loops, hidden belts and cinches that could be tightened for walking and loosened for staying in one place. It could be arranged in a way that daylight would pour out, or folded so that the stars and moon would catch its edges and make it seem as if the wearer was hovering against the backdrop of night.

It was too complicated a cloth and I felt unworthy, not knowing its tricks and intimacies, and moreover, it was more cumbersome than one would think. It could not be worn within a mile of the ocean lest salt-infested wind meet the fabric and loosen a stitch. It could not be worn at too high an altitude where the fabric would strain towards the too-thin air and unbalance the tension of its composition.

I am wearing this robe and running from my enemies, the forest is thick with brambles and the bamboo groves and underbrush are unkind. The impossible cloth is falling away as my feet begin to ache and burn, a rainbow-coloured crane flies off my left shoulder into the air, a jade-green frog leaps from right pocket to sink into the mud, a thread caught on a torn branch pulls off a speckled grey locust.

In a small clearing, what is left is unrecognisable. I will later burn what remains, sift through the ashes for ivory buttons and gold thread which I will use to barter for new clothes.

I told a fortune teller about my dream; he poured fragrant tea into a rice bowl and examined the patterns of tiny black stems and leaves. "Your children will not learn to write the old language, and their children will not learn to speak it. You will live to see them but not be able to converse."

~

Years ago, I did not know a single person who was similarly marked by love of someone of the same sex. I made up my own theories and explanations, which stayed in my head, background chatter which would sometimes surface, but was never actually spoken aloud. When I finally told friends of my attractions, they didn't fully understand what it meant, but were kind enough. I knew I had chosen my friends well.

Still, I noticed that I moved quite easily into different social circles. I hung out with various groups in the early years of high school, and then came into a time when my friends were mostly kind-hearted male heterosexuals. I wanted their normality to rub off on me, their easy testosterone-laden cologne, the comfort which they wore their gestures. On the right person, their genuine astonishment and disappointment at the world's cruelties had a charmed innocence which I had lost long ago. I developed wild crushes on them which I never revealed.

After that, I fell into a period of women friends, also straight. I appreciated the bells in their voices, the mystery of their internal world. I connected with their anger at subtle and not-so-subtle misogyny, their occasional world-weariness. Besides, we could man-watch together and compare notes on boyfriends.

It was in those days that I noticed the start of a gay vocabulary. They *flirted*, gay men *cruised*. They stared at *buttocks, cheeks, buns*. We stared at *a hot ass*. They called each other *girlfriends* and I was their *gay friend*. I would call them *women friends* (never having had a girlfriend) and called myself *queer* and sometimes for effect, *faggot*, a name they could not call me, nor would I want them to.

By the time I moved into a circle of gay friends (with the occasional lesbian), the gap in language was now a crevice.

Camp was not a place but an attitude, *drag* more adjective and noun than verb. On forays into the straight world, I caught myself saying *fabulous* and calling the people I was with *dear* and *darling*.

There were other words and phrases that sounded odd and attention-seeking outside of my circle: *piercing, cock-ring, rimming, park sex, bathhouse, glory hole*. A *gay bashing* was not like a birthday bash. Darker words too: *combo therapy, T-cells, Ritonavir, AZT, Kaposi's sarcoma, pneumocystis*.

I had lost language to talk with old friends, I had immigrated from one circle to another, and the old language, the one I had been brought up with, did not always do. Suddenly, I was unable to talk of what I'd seen. And while I had changed circles before, I felt that this was the one in which I would stay.

~

They were rough with us and though I did not understand the words they were saying, I could feel their disdain and insult. I had seen one or two white devils in my life before arriving. I found their skin porous and the colour of death, a dark mass of hair on their faces below the surface, struggling to get out. Some had tufts of curled wiry hair sprouting from tops of sleeves and shirts. Hair, hair, all over. I found it sometimes hard to tell them apart. After a few days we knew them, like eyes adjusting in the darkness:

the mean ones, the ones without expression, the ones with metal in their voices, the ones with coal.

Maybe it was the same for them, but I don't think so. We were too many to tell apart, crammed into small spaces, metal and concrete prisons, although they called it a "waiting station" where we languished days and weeks before we were allowed to officially set foot on Gold Mountain. We scraped poems into the walls with nails and rock, the white men brought us mysterious tasteless food, told us where to go, and sometimes gave us passage to the place we'd been travelling to, before we were stopped and numbered and held by their rules and regulations.

~

It was the centre of the city that I saw as my entrance, the dense grids of glass and concrete, electricity wires and flashing lights hiding worlds upon worlds, different countries.

In a vast run-down bookshop in a gritty part of downtown, I chose and bought my first pornographic magazine. I'd been looking for old science-fiction paperbacks and had been drawn to the corner of the store where the eyes of the men looking out from the covers of magazines were like traffic lights that said RED (stop or you'll get hit), YELLOW (caution, slow down), GREEN (go, go as fast as you can before they tell you to stop again).

I riffled through the pages and the blood shifted to different parts of my body; the back of my throat opened and became dry. I chose the one with the glossiest photos, hairless men, like me, no uniforms since I had never liked policemen, nor moustaches which I thought at the time looked ridiculous on anybody. The man at the counter gave me an ugly look to go with the brown paper bag for the magazine.

The men in the magazine were magnificent, of course, sleek and rounded all at once, expansive wide chests and ridged abdominal muscles. Big in every way, skin hues of pink and white and bronze, grey tones for black and whites, red and shadow browns for colours. So overcome by heat that I never stopped to dissect the camera's tricks: cheekbones made mountain ridges, pupils of eyes made oceans, men of five foot nothing made to look six foot two.

The images were outside of reality and outside of me, unattainable and far away. I could not imagine these objects of desire in my world and could not imagine, on the basis of these polished white gods, that I would ever be an object of desire.

Downtown held discos as well as bookstores, doorways of promise lit from above, garish posters and advertisements of the week's events posted alongside. Inside this portal was a second one, double Cerberus, a face through a window or burly t-shirted doormen.

The passage was variable: I could be waved through or stopped. Maybe they asked if I knew what kind of club it was. This mystified me: did I look as if I had accidentally walked in off the street? How could they not see the seething bundle of desire and hope that I was? Why wasn't I recognisable as someone who would go to the club? Other times, they would hold my driver's license up to the light and squint at the year of birth. This irritated me. Apologetic grin. "I can never tell the age of Orientals." Not that I can either, all the time, but always this extra test. And no, I don't look nineteen.

I have many stories about doorkeepers, even of complicity when their colour of skin is dark like mine. There are times though – too often – when flesh and blood become bigger, become simultaneously ethereal and more solid. So that guards are no longer needed and it is we that bar the gates to others hoping to immigrate to our countries.

~

Don't envision the place we gather. Hear it. A flock of ivory ducks all speaking at once. The day when the rain came in wooden blocks. It is a sound of clacking multiplied until each square of the room is occupied with more than one syllable. This is the sound when we gather to play mah-jong, the tiles being mixed, dancing together.

We smoke tobacco, drink whiskey, and gamble. When the evening has ripened some, we eat plates of barbecued pork and white steamed chicken. We give each other names, some known to the recipients and others not. This one is Shovel, the shape of his chin and his flat pallet face.

That one is Snoots because of the way he sticks his lower chin out and curls his nose down at the same time. This other one is called Stupid. Sometimes I can't even remember what his name was before.

We talk about the old country, the way things tasted, the smell of the morning in the village when the season turned. Sometimes we talk about the people we left behind and who we hope to bring to Canada. Brother. Wife. Daughter. Son.

We talk about how we first heard about this country, across the wide palm of the ocean. Did a friend or neighbour first speak of it? Did the idea spontaneously arrive in the head, a sudden sparrow alighting on a branch? Was the decision to go immediate or a slow turning, like leaving red beans to ferment to make into spice?

People have died here for missing their old homes; a simple cough or fever escalated and suddenly they have crossed a bridge from endurance to despair. Who can blame them? Are we really happy in this new land? White devils treating us like village dogs. Work no easier than the old village but lacking the comfort of what is known.

In mah-jong, you match together tiles with the same patterns and take them from the centre. Seasons, directions and flowers can be matched with each other to make them disappear. This is what it seems like living in Gold Mountain, Gum Saan, looking for a land with gold dust in the wind. The seasons touch each other and disappear, the years pass, fly out of sight in different directions. We dream of home, not the way it was but the way we wished it was. We plan to send our bones there when we die.

~

It could be any youth group, support systems of five or ten or fifteen people in big or small cities, probably not in towns, maybe in a community centre, or an ill-furnished office or even someone's living room. We sit around and talk about where we came from, the schools we went to, the friends we lost, our first sexual experiences. We are linked because we are here together, because we have pulled up chairs from other tables to join with this one, because we all know each other's names.

We give each other new names too. Gerald becomes Mother because he runs around taking care of the other members of the group. John becomes Jane because he is Barbie-doll blond and effeminate and suggested the name in the first place. Monty becomes Mary, but run if you call him that. He hates it. Larry is called Chuckles because of the way his soft belly bounces when he laughs, which is often since he talks and laughs in equal parts.

This is a bad meeting. There is a new member, who none of us know very well, and we can't get him to stop crying. "I don't want it," he says in fragments. "I'm not like that. I want to go home." Tall gangly Kevin, his thin straw-coloured hair falling over his hands which are now covering his face. He's from a small farming community where he left his home and family behind; he finds it tough in a city. The old men in the bars wanted to make friends with him right away, and one, who seemed nicer than the rest, turned out worse than expected.

So we talk against the toughness of the world, against the tears, about how we first heard the word *gay*: childhood whispers, parents' jokes, preachers' condemnations, talk show radio. We swap stories about how we heard about the youth group: a sign on a bus, a help-line counsellor, a note posted in a gay bar, the phone book. Whether we marched right into our first meeting, or circled the block, ten, maybe twenty times first.

Kevin's crying has stopped and he is listening, his eyes not quite clean of tears. We'll worry about him, of course, like we worried about ourselves. People have died of grief missing their old homes, fallen into a hard crowd, done too many drugs, been sexually reckless.

Kevin looks at us, and the light of sad angels falls into the moisture in his eyes. "I want to live in the country. Have a simple life. Are there gay people in the country?" A smile en route to a joke but held back one step by hope and one step by grief.

"You can go wherever you want." Gerald, a.k.a. Mother, coos in a voice of down feathers. "But remember, no one sends you there. Make it your choice."

For one second, all of us in the circle see ourselves and each other walking to the places we've chosen.

~

I look up into the sky that is curved and shining and speckled with white. Like a reflection of the rising sun in the eye of a soaring hawk. There are borders laid down like bodies to rest, they reach out in a spiderweb like cracks in an eggshell, like the sound of shattering. These borders form islands and there are people on all of these islands. Some are visible but most are out of the line of sight, they are beyond the range of my eyes, even beyond that of the eyes of the hawk.

In my old country, I thought only of my old country. Now that I have entered this new land, it is not only here that I think of. I see in front of me all new lands, all of the different lands that exist, and do not exist, and float somewhere past the point where I can even imagine them.

~

This place, a camping spot, nestled into an island, Saltspring Island, is a favourite place. Now, here again after years away, it seems as if washed over by clouds and made anew. A pathetic fallacy, I think they call it, to believe that nature reflects my moods. It is not the place that is new again, but me. Still, if we give false attributes to ourselves and others, then why not to the sky and sea?

What does it mean to say that I am new? Once in philosophy class, our teacher, Dominique, a Québecoise with a seventies coif, a lilting accent and tortoise shell eyeglasses, taught us the theory that what is false is the belief that we are one person throughout our lives who changes and grows and sheds skin; instead we are simply bundles of emotions and thoughts and short-term memory that link ourselves to ourselves. Agree or disagree? I will tell you my version: that it was always there, this love of men and love for men, and that now, it is like the boy who knew he could swim but never saw water, was never in water deep enough to float even, to push out arms into the soft hydrogen oxygen belly and pull them back towards himself. Now, there is water.

I am walking and I come to the edge of a lake. I stoop, feeling shifts and strains in my muscles and bones. I pick up the first rock that I see that is as large as my fist. I drop it on my image in the water. It splits into many images and then vibrates like a school of tiny herrings scattering at the sensation of danger.

I take my clothes off, shoes, shirt, pants, underwear. Don't forget the watch. The reflection in front of me shows trees on the shoreline, the sky getting darker, a hint of orange on the horizon like a stack of newspapers left in the sun changing colour. I anticipate the cold, the senses activated all at once, the complete submersion. My knees bend, and I spring forward.

When I dive into the water, it is because I have left the

air behind. I breathe blue oxygen through my nostrils and lungs, my hair floats away like tiny jellyfish, I rise into the air, which is also blue. I am alive two times. Seven times. Every shade of blue is a new country, a new lifetime.

Almost Flying

When Ayumi thinks of Australia, she thinks first of her own country, Japan, as a small round pebble, hard and ancient. Unchangeable. She has thrown the stone into a lake, and here, one of the far ripples is Australia, a thousand times larger, edges shimmery and not fully formed, a new land.

Her first arrival: everything that was different took her away from herself. No endless circlings of the self, a dog chasing its tail. Here her eyes were directed outwards: frangipani, yellow singing itself out from the centre of blossoms; ibis, an unfamiliar bird, long hooked beak like a sabre; fruit bats overhead, adorning the sky at dusk.

She was a mere girl of nineteen and the escape lasted one year: three hundred and sixty-five days exactly that started with Ayumi as a Japanese school girl in bobby socks and barrettes and ended with a young woman dressed in a sleek black dress and a slight wobble to her heels, but style in the sweep of her hair, strength in the carriage of her shoulders, and something in her eyes that wasn't there before.

Could she leave it behind? It was here where she was drunk for the first time, the lights of Sydney's Bondi Beach pulsing around her, the crowd at night swaying to a new rhythm. Reckless: sleeping on a park bench once, short of money, travelling up to the Gold Coast by bus. It was also the first time Ayumi had travelled alone, aside from the flight from Tokyo to Sydney. But this was different. In the plane, she was bound by the curved plastic walls around her, strapped into the rose-red seats. Outside: sky and clouds and only the direction that gravity would pull her. But here beyond the windows of the rattling bus were all directions, country that stretched like soft candy, out and out and out. A first kiss: not yet. But she'd gotten close, and oh, how she knew that it would come, someday.

School was less successful. While she spoke English in slow precise tones that were clear and understandable, it was too much of a leap to her courses in English literature. And even if she would return to Japan speaking English better than most of her old university classmates, she was unsure of where to use her new education.

After the whirlwind last month of travelling as far and as long as she could to see more of the giant island, she returned home, wondering how she would explain to her parents that she'd failed half of her courses, but that it didn't really matter. It really didn't.

~

To *hope* and to *dream* are the same word in Japanese. So when Ayumi wants to tell someone about her bad dreams, she wonders if they'll think that she's asking for misfortune. But there's no one to talk to about them. When she returned to Osaka, she suddenly realised that there were few of her old friends she wanted to see. Over coffee and cake (she'd forgotten how expensive it was here!) with one of them, they talked about studying, the city, old classmates. "Have you seen kangaroos? Did you go to Ayers Rock? Did you try surfing? How was the weather?" Never about the new weather inside her.

Her parents, as before, did not speak to each other; it was when she was seven years old that sharp words and shouting had suddenly become blank space in the air, a row of windows with panes missing. Her ears take time to readjust to the silence. It is like the quiet in the oldest temples.

So, the dreams stay inside her head and haunt her daytime: Japanese *manga* characters stumbling through the sets of Australian and British soap operas; loud surfers and lifeguards dashing through Japanese rock gardens and temples; sushi bars with glass counters filled with plastic replicas of burgers and chips; geisha girls in ill-fitting two-piece bathing suits. Falling in and out of her nights.

Her mother is worse than before, she seems to be talking to herself lately, and there's an anger that follows her, a bird that hovers behind her neck and shoulders. Her father is nowhere in sight, arrives home late, says little. Her brother has left home a few months ago for Singapore to become an evangelical Christian minister. Ayumi is a little surprised by this but sees it as the conclusion of his conversion three years ago: the sudden appearance in the house of neat packs of religious pamphlets and papers, a bible next to his futon.

Now alone with her parents, she knows already that she won't be able to continue with university: the ordered studying, high-pressure exams, the mass of students all headed in the same direction. What is her direction? She's acquired a wilful weakness, a great stretch of night desert inside of her that wakes and sleeps to its own rhythm.

Her schedule becomes this: work, when she can get it. Housework afterwards, assisting her mother. At night, she writes letters to her friends in Australia, and marvels at the place names in the addresses. Wollongong, Canberra, Coogee. Her letters are short: two or three pages, written in careful square handwriting on delicate sheets of rice paper, or silly feminine stationery in pinks and blues with button-eyed cartoon characters. The writing paper is left-over from before she left Japan, but she knows if she goes to buy new supplies, the designs will be pretty much the same. She always starts the same way: *How are you??* Then a few short paragraphs: something happening in the city, perhaps the weather, a number of questions, and a few lines to say that she is working, or reading, or helping her mother around the house.

It's only after a few months that the content changes. "I am too tall and fat and have marks on my face. Someone in the street called me ugly the other day. People stare, and my boss asked me to try and do something about it." Or this: "I left my job at the bookstore. It did not feel like useful work, bowing to customers and wrapping their purchases. I couldn't speak with the other working girls who were always giggling and gossiping."

Ayumi goes through a number of jobs during this period: parking lot attendant, grocery store clerk, shop assistant at a department store. She also spends much time looking at herself in the mirror. She isn't really overweight but she is tall, and compared to the tiny-boned women she sees on the street, she feels monstrous, ungainly.

Plus she has beauty marks. Ironic for her when she learned the English phrase, since the Japanese consider them unattractive. And unlucky, like a constellation of broken stars. "I don't know what to do. I don't like life very much. Sometimes, I wonder what it would be like to die."

Her friends write back to her quickly. They suggest counsellors (she knows none); psychologists (who are only for the truly sick); going back to university (after she'd already dropped out); and physical activity (girls do not exercise). Also, taking up hobbies, trying to make more friends, support from her family.

~

When she first awakes, eyes slowly opening, pupils dilating in the bright light, her first words are "Not high enough." Another failure, really. She isn't one of those just trying to get attention. Six stories should have been enough.

Ayumi realises that she does not understand the human body very well: a broken hip and leg, fractures in her wrist and arm. What would it have taken? She had expected the jump to be clean, quick, and eventually, painless.

Instead, the healing takes months. Trapped in a hospital bed surrounded by nurses who make her feel small and pathetic with their false sympathy. At least she has a routine, something to do during the long hours in the hospital: meals orderly and on time, regular appointments for physiotherapy. She doesn't really mind. Her favourite time is late at night: compact noises of heel against polished floor, an occasional click from beds or chairs being wheeled down the hall, a soft buzz of machine and lights, and everywhere, breathing, in and out, out and in.

~

Over the next seven years, Ayumi works intermittently, never more than four or five months at a time. Then she has periods of reading, wandering the streets during the day, endless cleaning and polishing in the house. Her letters to friends become less frequent but return to the style of her first correspondence: informative and cordial. Her correspondents are relieved at this. They wonder if the peace will last, but are content to receive letters with less anxiety than before.

They do not receive news about Ayumi's mother. In fact, they know nothing of her family: her silent businessman father who barely seems alive; her brother who has returned infrequently, only three times, to visit the family since leaving for Singapore; her mother who has deteriorated, at times quickly, other times slowly.

This is what has taken up most of Ayumi's time. She does the majority of cooking, cleaning and shopping and is in charge of the home without quite realising it. Her mother has nervous attacks, and becomes delusional and nonsensical. Sometimes, Ayumi checks her into the mental ward of the local hospital. It is an odd routine yet she knows that it is not only the body that is resilient, but the mind as well. She no longer worries about what she looks like. She has enough to fill her days.

When she has enough savings, enough to stay in Australia for nearly a year, she does not request permission of her father to leave, she announces it. His expression as always gives little away but her eyes widen when he later places in her hands enough money to last for at least another six months. He advises her to find a good exchange rate for the yen. She prepares to leave.

~

Now, back in Australia for nearly six months: the birds, bats, beaches are all the same, as is the magnificent Harbour Bridge and the sails of the Sydney Opera House. She walks for hours at a time, visiting all of her favourite spots. She is pleasantly surprised that many of her university friends have stayed in Sydney, never to return to live in the towns they were born in. She sees them and they comment on how good she looks. After a month in a youth hostel in King's Cross, she finds a job as a live-in nanny for a young Australian-Japanese couple with a quiet two-year-old boy, Taro, still young enough to be good-natured and easy to care for.

~

She hears him before she sees him, talking to it seems like anybody in the hall, the rooms. The hostel is busy, filled with the rowdy energy of backpackers chatting and trading travel tips. She has kept mostly to herself, as she retraces old walks and relearns the sounds of the city, but soon she is drawn into his conversation, his energy. Martin. She mistakes him at first for American, then later recognises his soft quirkiness and round vowels as Canadian. He has a rugged unkempt look about him that makes her smile. He is a colouring book picture with spills over the lines. She can picture the stares he would attract in Japan.

It is a quick romance. This is the end of his trip rather than the beginning. Martin has travelled through Australia in a rickety car with a crazy Dane he'd left behind in Perth, and a reserved Englishman who has only recently departed. They'd driven to Alice Springs and Cairns and later even ferried across to Tasmania. After two months in Sydney, Martin has made a bit more travel money working at a call centre, though he's sick of answering questions about mobile phones. Tahiti and Fiji are the next stops before heading back to Kingston.

That's where he grew up, on a dairy farm on the outskirts of a small city outside of Toronto. Where he acquired the wide-eyed wonder of someone from the country, and the habit of saying "youse" for the plural form of "you." *How are youse doing?* His long light-coloured hair and traveller's stubble make her think he looks a bit like Kurt Cobain. For a joke, she tells him that her name is Ayumi Love.

A hot and humid afternoon, he takes her hand and swings it forward then back. The joints and muscles in his arms are fluid as water; her arm pulled along awkwardly, straining against her shoulder's socket. Even when the other schoolgirls would link arms and join on the pavement into a small train of dark blue uniforms, Ayumi had managed to stay apart.

Now she is joined and feels a shift in the rhythm of the swing. She glances up into Martin's pensive eyes as their arms cease motion.

"What was it like?"

It takes her a moment to understand, like eyes adjusting to the darkness. Then she hears an echo finally returned from a distant place. He was speechless when she first told him her secret, silent for a long time afterwards. Now it's her turn without words. While she knows what he's referring to, she doesn't know which part. The takeoff, the fall, the landing? Inside her head or the rushing sky around her?

~

After two months together, Ayumi takes the bus with him to the airport. She waits quietly until the last possible moment before he has to go through the customs gates. He cradles her head with his forearms, his hands resting on the crown of her head. When she looks up, she is surprised to find him crying, his freckled skin has turned red and wet with tears. She does not cry but instead looks at him with amazement.

When they speak on the phone a week later, he tells her that he will be sending an airline ticket for her, as soon as he's made enough money. He doesn't know that she could pay for the ticket for herself. She'll wait though, not for the ticket, though she'll use it if it arrives, but for the proof that he's serious in his offer.

In the meantime, she plays with young Taro under an Australian sun, and wonders what Canada is like. Martin told her it's much like Australia but colder and with fewer beaches. She wonders if he's told his parents about her, and forms a long daydream in her imagination about sitting in a warm Canadian kitchen with the family. His father is talkative and wants to know about Japan. Martin's mother wants to know about Australia. They laugh together, they bring out Martin's photo collection from his travels.

Ayumi is recalling a day together at the zoo, animals she'd never seen before, a warm buzzing inside of her like the wings of a nocturnal bird. Martin grabs her wrist, guides her hand up in front of him. It's an awkward gesture; she guesses that he'll tell her something. Westerners spill out occasional confidences like the tide leaving behind treasure on a beach front.

"I knew you from when I first saw you. Everything you've said confirms that I'm right."

She holds back from nodding her head for she knows it would be false. Somewhere inside of her understands. The rest of her isn't so sure.

"Fall for me, Ayumi. Will you do that?"

He didn't get a response then, and it may be a while before her echo follows her out into the open air. The echo from the answer in her head when he asked her that question.

For now, she hopes Martin won't tell anyone her secret and come to think of it, especially not his parents. All of her foreignness, from gesture to jet-black eyelashes, will probably be enough for them already. One day though, she expects that she'll have been out of Japan so long, the old country will fall off, a silk kimono fallen to the ground. On will come new clothes, and maybe she'll even try out how it feels to confess like a North American, open herself like a spring bloom. Maybe that day, she'll tell them how close to flying it was.

Sleep

I can't sleep.

The room is stuffy like too many thoughts at once. Hot like a crowded amphitheatre. Even though it's just me, opening the door to the balcony, trying to let some air in. Third floor, heat rising.

The crickets drone in rhythmic pulses, and the shape of the street that faces the bedroom catches echoes from far and near: a loud revving engine, the automatic garage door down the way, the grumbly drunks across the street in social housing, a whistle, a horn.

If I had them, I'd put in earplugs but I've forgotten to buy another pack. Six perfect small fat flexible cylinders, packed perfectly like a half dozen eggs. Squeeze the styrofoam material, shove them in, and instead of night noise, you hear the sound of your heart and lungs from the inside out. During the course of the evening though, they fell out, rolled under the pillow or cover, down under the bed, into a dust bunny in the corner. Lost, one by one, each and every. So, no earplugs.

I was sleeping earlier tonight in a breezy first-floor room, a high ceiling like you find in Europe, a pristine tall uncluttered box of a room, lights with dimmers set to low. Granted, the voices of neighbours through the open back door woke me from time to time. Did they hear our moans and shortened breaths?

Patrick had no problem sleeping, his long arm comfortably bent into an L and resting over me. It was his height that attracted me, forced to look up as these grey eyes bore down upon me. My glance shifted slightly down onto a mouth that widened suddenly into a goofy infectious grin with good strong teeth. Just below that, a patch of hair below the lip and above the chin. A jazz patch, I'd heard it called until someone told me it's an imperial. A good look.

I could have slept there, awoken with morning light filtering down through the windows in the back doors, watched shadows uninterrupted by fixture or furniture slowly shift on the walls. Shook the sleep off, thinking of coffee or orange juice or Irish Breakfast tea.

The bedsheet was just the right weight too. I could feel it was expensive. Cotton threads balanced perfectly on a loom, designed to cover you like an eyelid does an eye.

Or maybe it was just the weight of his arm, settled, warm

but dry. His chest was broad and torso thick, but his limbs were elegant and light. I could have slept in that cradle.

My comforter (*doona*, they say here) is too heavy for this weather, but the bedsheet is too light – it's worn and thin in places, and I wonder how old it is. Have you ever realised that the pieces of lint collected in the filter of your dryer are your clothes slowly dissolving every time they go through a cycle? This sheet has been washed many times. Sweat and other bodily fluids infused and removed regularly.

I have to have something over me to sleep. Open air disturbs my skin, which is why I can't sleep nude either. Although I wish I could. I remember pyjamas, soft flannel for the winter, thin light cotton for the summer, mother would decide the change in season. I was in high school when I stopped wearing them. Ascertained that a t-shirt and underwear were what teenage boys slept in.

I turn on the bedside lamp and plug in a mini-fan/heater which I bought because Sydney is much colder in the winter than the tourist board would have you believe. This is the first time I've tried it in summer. I set it to cool, leave it running. But it's far too noisy.

It's only recently that I've noticed how many people have trouble sleeping. Droopy-eyed colleagues, if you pry, they've had a bad night too. Maybe it's this hot weather, the natives can't get used to it either.

Surprisingly, Eric has been sleeping well lately, though he e-mailed me that he was a little horny after the last time we talked and couldn't sleep afterwards. Eric has a terrible complex about sleeping with people, which is when he really has problems. He would lie awake next to Craig. Four years of staring at the ceiling, worried about waking up his partner. Sometimes he'd crawl out and try to sleep on the floor. Nothing would work. Chamomile tea, honey and milk, herbal pills, sleeping tablets: he tried them all. The worst part was the spiral: getting more and more upset at not being able to sleep, agitation levels rising, the heartbeat stepping up into a daytime rhythm, so that sleep became impossible.

It may have been why they broke up in the end. When pressed, Eric admits, "Maybe I never trusted him enough."

It may be the reason why he fell for me, for the night after we made love, which was different from the first times which were just sex, we both decided without admitting it that we liked one another. After a perfect twin orgasm, we fell simultaneously into a deep sleep and woke ten hours later.

~

I must be out of my mind getting involved in a long-distance relationship. I'd always said I never would. Whopping phone bills, airport goodbyes, time apart. The worst is your mind only half being where you are and half far away.

However, since Eric wasn't living in Sydney, I didn't even think of the possibility of a relationship when we met. I let my guard down and when I tried to put it up, I realised I hadn't met anyone who had affected me in quite the same way for a very long time.

His relationship with Craig had ended poorly. They'd drifted apart and had completely stopped having sex, but Eric was still expected to be faithful.

With me, he says, let's see how it goes, have sex with other people when we're apart, take things day by day. Sleep on it, he told me. But I'd already agreed.

It's two hours ahead of Sydney in Auckland and he's probably dreaming, REM – the eyes darting around behind the eyelids like goldfish in a bowl, goldfish on amphetamines. In last week's newspaper I read about dreams, the latest theories. One said that the brain needs to flush out metabolic wastes. This action creates hallucinations, i.e., dreams. Another one says that the brain simply needs to practise for being awake. It grabs random thoughts from present and past, orders them any way it wants, and puts them together. Dreams: they apparently don't mean anything at all.

Patrick, a few blocks away, must be asleep as well. I'm jealous of his heavy sleep, he didn't even rouse as I lifted his arm up and slid off the king-size mattress. Put on my clothes, found a pad of paper, and wrote "Thx Patrick. Talk soon. M." Though in the dark and my drowsiness the middle letters in "talk" ran together into a strange shape. I think he'll understand in the morning. The "a" and the

"I". And that staying overnight on the first date might mean too much of a commitment, as would writing "enjoyed dinner" or "it was a lovely evening."

As Eric knows, sometimes the more you try to sleep, the more you end up thinking. Same thing with meditation: you're trying to clear your head and can't stop thinking that your head is not clear. So, the objective, though it doesn't help at the time to remember it, is simply to do it. Sleep. Meditate.

I was worried that when I met Patrick for dinner I'd spend so much time thinking about not talking that talking is all I'd do. But I didn't. I just did it. Went out with him. Made amiable conversation. Kissed him when I couldn't resist. Proud too, that I held back the torrent of talk, of confession.

The main thing of course that neither of us asked each other about was boyfriends and relationships. Me assuming that a man of his experience wouldn't expect that I'm single just because I called him up and asked him out to dinner. Just because I'd passed up dessert and said, "Let's go back to your place." At least not in Sydney. Assuming, I mean.

But also that I held back from telling him about when we met. He said, "We've met before." I said, "On the dance floor." And we talked about where it might have been. But what I could have confessed and said too much about was that the only memory I have from however many months ago was looking up and seeing him and thinking "sex." Sex. And he smiled. Maybe for five minutes, maybe twenty – you never know on Ecstacy. Then he disappeared. Or I did. The last I saw of him.

Until this weekend. He comes into the bar and I looked over at him and didn't look away. Words like "brazen," "uncool," "patently obvious" come to mind, but he played it fine, nodded and talked to others, including friends of mine, before I finally introduced myself, said, "We've met before," before he excused himself, he had some work to do. When he left, I asked Tabish right away: "Is Patrick single?"

The answer I wanted: "No. He's in a long-term relationship. But they're both allowed to fool around and Patrick likes having sex with guys who look kind of like you."

The answer I got: "Yes, he's single." Big grin and laughter in the voice. "And he's looking. And he asked after you." Beat. "I'll give you his phone number."

My friend Adam in London would go nights and nights without sleeping, his eyes became wider and wider during this period, sometimes, when talking to him, a light would seem to switch off, and without even blinking, it would seem he had fallen asleep and woken up in the same second. If you didn't know he had insomnia, you'd just think he was a bit dizzy. I couldn't imagine what it would be like to not sleep like that. It was affecting his relationship too. Boyfriend Ben was getting pretty frustrated, and on top of that, they were negotiating monogamy.

Ga-na-ma-knee, I'd say facetiously. Get on my knee. Or if there's a threesome, all of whom are faithful to each other, it would be trigonometry, wouldn't it?

But the truth was that I'd not had to deal with it. A singleton, bachelor boy, eternally non-coupled, that was me, I could never find what I was looking for. I reasoned that when I did, I would be inundated with interesting men. For that's the rule: when you wash the car, it rains; when you're in a relationship, people besides your boyfriend court you; when you're single, you're single. So, it made sense that just when I'd found someone who I really really liked, who it must be said, didn't and doesn't live in the same city, that someone else who is interesting would come along. Like Patrick.

I sometimes wonder about people who work night shifts. How they move against the traffic, alter their internal clock, discover a small nation of people of like minds or situation. They're awake now, in all-night cafés, convenience stores, gas stations and hospitals. I've joined in their waking state.

Maybe I'll try to have a nap later today. Though I've never napped well. I fall into too deep a sleep and when awoken, feel more tired than before. Wander around in a groggy daze until logic and social norms say it's an acceptable time to retire to bed. Some of these norms you listen to; some you don't. Standard behaviour says that I should be with women not men. Heterosexual rules say, stick with what you've got, don't play the field. Representatives of all sexualities break these rules.

I wonder what rules Patrick breaks. Also, whether he has long or short relationships, whether he has had many at all, whether he became friends with them after they broke up, whether he always sleeps so well, what side of the bed he prefers, whether he likes to sleep alone.

Lastly, I wonder if Patrick will turn into a good friend, if the first romp in the sack will change into something quieter. Or what if this thing doesn't work out with Eric, and I've passed up meeting Patrick, and by the time Eric and I break up, Patrick is with someone else? Or what if this turns into a mad romance, and I'm simply put into one of those circumstances where a choice has to be made?

I am certain that if Eric were in the same city, I'd be playing house with him and seeing him regularly. I'd tell him if I was going to have sex with someone else, and we'd agree to only have sex with other men who were sexy but uninteresting, picked up in saunas and bars.

I've often wondered if I'd ever be able to sleep through the night with someone else by my side. I'm usually too restless to sleep well after sex. No wonder. I made naked contact those first years after nearly escaping my entire teenage years without so much as a wet kiss. How could my heart not be clanging against my sleep box, in someone else's bed, someone else's home, maybe someone else's city? All those first affairs were not just sex, they were the world about to begin, they were how much of the world there was to explore. More recently, if I was with someone, I would wake repeatedly during the night. Maybe I've really gotten used to sleeping alone. What amazes me is couples that I've met that have gotten so used to sleeping together that they can't sleep apart. Now that's co-dependence.

So it surprised me how well Eric and I slept together. Most nights of the first week we met. And then every night of the five days I visited him, two weeks ago. Even if Eric did have trouble sleeping one or two of those nights, he told me that I didn't notice him getting up out of bed and coming back in. I slept right through.

How long does it take to get used to someone so you can sleep with them? I never liked one-night stands, for somewhere deep inside I worried about my safety. Axe-murderers and crazies. Having a stranger in your bed until the morning, or being in a strange apartment. Though some men much prefer this to quick encounters in parks or saunas. Maybe that's the point, some people don't need to get used to others. Or some people you don't need to get used to. You already are.

"If you love somebody," the saying goes, "set them free."

"If they don't come back," says the parody, "hunt them down and kill them."

Sleep on *that*.

I'd go with the first thought. I'd like to believe that if you're truly meant to be with someone, if the other person needs to test it, then he should. If he doesn't come back, it will hurt but it's the right choice. I know this idea is romantic and perhaps unrelated to how real life works.

On the other hand, at least I know what I want. It's not often that you meet someone and know that you're going to get somewhere. I meet men every day that I want to sleep with, which isn't saying much. Sydney is overfilled with them. Everyone admits that it's excessive. And I meet men at times and we both want to sleep with each other. Every once in a while. But it's the less-frequent-than-every-once-in-a-while times. Maybe twice a year, or less, though that's a complete guess. The times when you actually think, there's something more.

I consider those times like being on a trip through the wildest lands of your imagination: deserts and plains, jungles and grassland. Unexpectedly, you glimpse the most unusual bird, or the strangest animal, a gift to say that sometimes you've just got to take notice of how rare the world can be. Drink it in.

I don't know it now, of course, no premonitions on this sleepless night, but Eric will leave me in two months for someone else. I won't talk to him for months afterwards.

Patrick, I'll see from time to time, the same infectious grin and warm greeting, but we never socialise for more than a few minutes at a time and we never become friends.

But now? Lying on my stomach instead of my back, I'm turning thoughts over in my mind. Eric is far away, sleeping in another time zone. Patrick is sleeping in this one. I'm wide awake thinking that I'm far too used to getting what I want, or what I think I want.

And I'm wondering if I'd stayed the night in Patrick's bed, whether I'd be fast asleep by now, having dreams that don't mean anything at all.

Signs

Neal found my ad. Gay dating *fin-de-siècle*: you sign on to the Web, click onto the page, post your ad, and men respond. From there, you can exchange e-mails, and for the more technologically advanced, photos, electronic ones that dissolve into pixels and reassemble on someone else's screen.

I said: Looking for that elusive "one" but open to meeting friends, lovers, and fuck-buddies along the way. I want to meet someone with the right "click" and energy, a good conversationalist. Someone interested and engaged with the world with a healthy attitude towards themselves and relationships, whether they are casual or serious. Physically I have a weakness for handsome rather than cute.

He replied: handsome, single, sane and busy professional who loves travel and indulges often. I enjoy a wide range of music, film, theatre, and partying in moderation. Am water-mad and love a fast sail, a fast ski, and even faster cars. Long languid meals, the intimacy of exploring a partner and waking entwined. Staring at art, exploring a half-built house, the afternoon haze over the harbour through a long cool drink. Looking for honesty and a sense of discovery and fun.

I said I was interested.

He sent me a photo.

I sent him a photo and my phone number.

He called.

We arranged to meet.

On the first date, what I liked about Neal was his self-effacement, as if he was trying to impress me rather than I him. I like a bit of effort. I think it's a good sign. He talked quickly but with silence in between, a morse code I was comfortable with. I talked. He talked. A conversation.

I'm conservative, he told me, and I didn't know what that meant. Politically conservative, I might have had problems with though opposites can attract. Financially conservative: well, who cares? I deduced that he was socially conservative, someone contained within himself. Like a clock, the interior an ordered complexity, a simpler face shown to the world. When I asked, he explained himself to be measured and not too wild.

We had coffee and dessert at a café, split the bill, then walked underneath leafy green trees, past terrace houses, some lit inside, others dark. We were both tired from work. It wasn't going to be a late night.

Sometimes it's awkward asking people what they do. It might seem like you're looking for something in particular. I'm not. But I want to know people who like their work and if they don't, can tell me what they really like to do.

I was on a date with this French guy who lamented, "Americans. You're always asking about jobs right away. It's so crude." Fine, I thought. Your ball. Ask me a question. He never did.

Me, I work for AIDS organisations. They're usually poor. They pay a moderate salary. I work in countries other than my own. The money I save goes towards airfares to visit my family and paying for periods when I'm not working. While I work in AIDS policy and education and have friends who are HIV-positive, I forget what it must be like to live with the disease. People tell me: That's great what you do. Wow. Well done. That must be really tough.

In fact, I sit in front of a computer and a telephone most days. I think about concepts more than individual faces.

Neal does AIDS research. He used to treat patients in a general practice at the same time. These days, it's studies and clinical trials. His institute is trying to find ways of making the drugs work better. Soon, they'll be involved in a project to develop a vaccine, something everyone is talking about.

He works too hard though. Sometimes, he talks about

being self-employed and dreams about working somewhere else in the world, maybe America. Maybe. Sometimes people's wishes-out-loud are not what they really want.

He'd worked with gay patients from the beginning, from the days we knew little about HIV and AIDS, through the long period of losing whole communities of men, to today's uncertainty and hope with advanced new treatments. Talking to him about this made my job seem more real.

Ex-boyfriends. Something I should learn to lie about. My longest relationship so far has been five months. Sometimes I say six instead, a rounder number, half a year, or half a dozen eggs neatly packed in their own carton. The rest I allude to: the first boyfriend that I never fell in love with; the one who stole my heart just as I was about to leave Brussels. My excuse is that I travel a lot, and am never in one place. Or that I'm choosy. Or that I need to find someone who is a match for me. I don't know how convincing I sound.

Neal, on the other hand, has a solid record. At least three relationships that lasted four years. A few other shorter ones. Cohabited often. Monogamous relationships all of them, which I find unusual these days, or maybe unusual in this city. He became friends with all of them except the last one, and sees them regularly. I treated this as a good sign.

Some dates I don't even get this far. You know right away there's nothing to talk about. If they're unusual enough to one day end up in one of my stories, I'll put in some time, ask questions, listen politely. Otherwise, a fast excuse and I'm out. I know I shouldn't tell him this but I do. Not the part about the stories, but how people are, by nature, self-centred.

He laughed, agreed and said, I don't date much. And you're the first date I've had from the Internet.

I invited him up to my apartment.

We sat on the couch, knees touching.

He told me that I have a beautiful neck.

I said that I loved his red hair.

That's good, he jested, since it's the only colour it comes in.

I would hear this joke again but in different variations: a deference and shunning of compliments – then a child's glee, and a satisfaction that the world had turned out that way, and was to his liking.

Tea in my apartment, out on the balcony. He said that he had to go. He was giving a presentation the next day to some medical students and wanted to review it.

What was it about?

He touched my bare arm. The skin, he explained, is the body's largest and most visible organ. Almost everyone who has HIV gets some sort of rash or infection. If you know how to read the signs correctly, you can identify not only a potential HIV symptom, but also how far the disease has progressed. Or, he said, sliding his hand up to my shoulder, it might be just a regular skin problem.

The tea was left to cool. We kissed without urgency and

arranged to see each other two days later. Since I usually sleep with men on the first date, or sleep with them before I make a first date, I thought it was a good start.

~

The second date, I jumped in aggressively. He had invited me to stay overnight at his place, an airy, bright house near Coogee Beach with a view of the water. Since I knew what was in store, I figured that long foreplay wouldn't hurt. I felt it was safe in the theatre in the back row, gay couples in the audience, someone just behind us to the left, and a gay performer doing a long monologue while a slide show played behind him, photos of his family relations around the world. The meaning of family and blood links. I grabbed Neal's hand, put it to my lips and made love to it.

Later at the restaurant, I tried to sneak a better look at his hands. I do this sometimes with dates as a trick, as a way to get them to talk more about themselves. Also, because I think there is some truth to palmistry, though I could never properly memorise what my cheap pocket guide had to tell me.

The problem was that most of the guys I date seem to have similar lines on their hands, so it was hard to come up with something new.

A long strong lifeline curving down into the wrist.

A headline in the middle stretching across the whole of

the palm, indicating many interests and the ability to go into different careers.

The heartline, the highest of the three, that's the important one. If it's curved, the person expresses his emotions better on the surface. If it's straight, the emotional life may be more hidden. The longer it is, the more romantic the person is, less jealous, more accepting of their partner, and more giving. Too long, though, and the expectations will be enormous. That's a person who would die for love. However, he somehow managed to keep his palms to himself for the whole time that I thought about palmistry.

Nearly everyone in Sydney is from somewhere else and Neal is no exception. But his family moved here from Melbourne when he was ten, so he considers that he's actually "from here." As proof, everyone knows Neal; he knows everyone. It's a big enough city to offer a good gay life, but not big enough to offer anonymity. I found out right away that he knew my friend Ross, as well as a host of others that I'd met since I'd arrived.

I have to admit that I felt uncomfortable knowing that if we started seeing each other, many friends would already know who he was. Rather than create a new history, I would have to fit into those of other people. As well, I would be noticed. *Who's Neal's new boyfriend?* Strange after fighting for so many years to share my love openly, the idea of a public relationship frightened me.

What I wanted to ask him was whether he believed in

true love. Is there a Romeo out there, or many Romeos? How many love aspects in a given astrological chart? What combination of physical, intellectual, spiritual and emotional is found in his affairs and relationships? Does he measure or guess the right amount of each one?

Instead I asked him what sign he was. I was surprised by the answer. I thought that Pisceans were supposed to be dreamers, impractical, preoccupied with their spiritual development. It's the sign on the chart closest to enlightenment. Granted, he likes the ocean and sea, so a water sign seemed appropriate, but he also likes fast cars, has a solid, respectable profession, and has a stubborn streak. An earth sign, I'd guessed.

Well, he explained, I'm impractical with money and buy new cars too quickly. Maybe that's the Pisces in me.

Neal is a traveller. I can't remember which signs of the zodiac like to travel. To survive the pressure of his heavy workload, he makes sure that he takes his full five weeks of annual leave every year. This year was a big one: a trip to Fire Island in New York; another one to London and Paris. Next year, he wants to do something more exotic, Portugal and Morocco maybe.

I try to remember the name of the most beautiful beach in the world. It's on the very southeastern tip of Portugal, just beyond the touristy southern strip of the Algarve. Far enough away that no one bothers to go except the handful of backpackers who had the same guidebook as I. Sleepy mornings, breakfasts of hard crusty rolls with salty butter and milky heart-starting coffee, grilled sardines and *vinho verde* for lunch.

The beach was below cliffs that wound around a coastline with the contours of jigsaw puzzle pieces. They rose straight up from the sands, tall and straight, a giant's toeprints in the earth. The ocean would sweep in and take away refuse. Leave a pristine surface, sand soft as a whisper and clean as a perfect meditation. *Sagres.* I didn't remember the name until after the last time we met.

From the theatre to the restaurant, Neal's driving had made me nervous, his bronze Mercedes-Benz dancing in and out of traffic, careening around corners as if in a game of tag. I can picture him renting a similar car, maybe in bright red, to drive up from Sagres north along the coast. Looking out for signs to take him to Lisbon.

Road signs fascinate me. If your eyes are half-closed, they could be the same anywhere in the world, white reflective lettering, variants of green background, warning signs in yellows, information in blues. But up close, there is something different, a shape of an arrow that you've never seen, a pictogram that you can't quite work out.

People make the mistake of saying that the world is the same all over, that wherever you go, whoever you meet, people are basically the same. Places and situations too. There is a difference, though, between something that is similar and something that is equivalent.

Take silhouettes of animals, for example. A shadow of a beast on a gold diamond can have several meanings: watch out for animals (so you can take photos if you're a tourist), watch out for animals (in case they suddenly appear in your headlights, try not to hit them), watch out for animals (you're out of the city now and anything could happen). So there is that basic truth: there are beasts in the wilderness the world over. Watch your step. At the same time, a moose is not like an elk, which is nothing like a kangaroo.

He grabbed the bill, which I don't like to happen on the first few dates, but I let him. My wallet was hurting at the time, and the restaurant he'd suggested was more expensive than I expected. He seemed to pay the bill out of generosity and pleasure rather than feeling sorry for me. He let me treat him to a much less expensive breakfast the next morning.

~

The third date was rollerblading in Centennial Park. Canadians are supposed to be able to ice-skate and ski. So when Neal said it's just like ice-skating, you're good at that, aren't you? I had to admit, No.

He veered from side to side on the path, moving from patience to impatience. My feet fell in too often, and I was far too cautious and self-conscious. I guess I only like speed when someone else controls it: roller coasters for example. When it's up to me it's steady as she goes.

C'mon, he coaxed, and we tried with me holding on to

his waist, then hands, which I only found more confusing. I noted that his desire for velocity had won over his natural discretion. This amused me, so I tried and did go faster but not by much.

Soon after, a cyclist in front of him slowed down abruptly. Neal cursed and swung out to the right on his blades and swivelled around to face my direction. His eyes lacked forgiveness. He bladed in silence a few moments, and then told me animatedly that a few weeks before, he'd done a marathon on these roller blades. A couple of hours it took him, quicker than if he ran. Some people might think of this as cheating, but I think it takes a certain amount of determination to do a marathon in any form.

~

Only three weeks later we had our last day together. We'd seen each other every few days since our first dates. It was not intense, but more than occasional. We spent the afternoon at Shelly Beach, quieter than nearby Manly, then drove to his home to wash up. The maid was coming the next day, and he spent the whole time I was in the shower tidying up. I joked with him about this. It had been a good, relaxed day. A day for teasing.

Well, sometimes I even follow her around and dust the places that she's missed. He looked up at me sheepishly. His red hair stood up in odd ways after a day outdoors. I was unsure if he was kidding or not.

I left to play bridge. I know this sounds old-fashioned but I do it every Sunday. I like to think of it as retro-cool. Afterwards, the four of us go to a local bar where we drink for longer than we played cards and dissect the day's strategies. That day, my partner and I lost the game and the bar was packed. The intermingling of smoke and sweat made me distracted and edgy.

Neal showed up to meet me. I saw him, left my friends standing around a small table and asked if he wanted to join us.

I've come to talk with you.

I turned towards him flattered and then saw the seriousness on his face.

These are the clichés he used: I'm not ready for a relationship. We don't want the same things. You're a real catch. I hope I wasn't leading you on. The click wasn't there.

Here's something that should be a cliché but I don't think is: I had to be honest.

This was his faux pas: The ad looked good.

Did you notice when we were making love?

Yes, but I thought it was holding back for better things. Letting anticipation grow. A prelude before a later symphony. No need to devour now because there is feasting tomorrow.

Instead, it was holding back.

I stayed in the bar after he left. The expression on my face a black eye that couldn't be disguised.

"Are you OK?" inquired Dean, a tall friendly acquaintance with an open comic-book face. "Three weeks, mate, that's not long. Plenty of fish in the sea."

How can I give my heart in such a short time? I know it's ridiculous.

Ross was next. "Well, since you're not going out with him now, I can tell you the bad things about him." When I'd found out that Ross knew Neal, I'd said, "Only tell me the good things." But now Ross nods and leans forward. "Physical abuse. A past history, with someone smaller than him. Like you. Better off without him."

I think of Neal and picture him in a lab coat, trying to find a combination of drugs safer and more effective for someone living with HIV. I imagine him in his earlier days of medicine, a daily schedule of caring, green eyes set in an expression of concern, a pink blush on his cheeks reflecting the red in his hair. How could he have done that? Hit someone. Hurt someone. And I remember him lifting me up in sex the first time we were together, the ease with which my weight rose into the air above his arms. I can see the power.

I've only been hit once in my life. Fourteen years old, a beachside park in Vancouver, and a pale wide-eyed girl in tattered jean jacket ran up, two older stronger boys with her who stood between me and my two friends.

"What did you say?" she demanded and started swinging, and while she was smaller and slighter than me, my arms were useless and remained lowered.

I couldn't hit a girl. Not even when she gave me a black

eye. Boys don't hit girls, I believed. Then again, I also thought: girls don't hit. Boys hit each other all the time. So do men. But with boxing gloves, or in bars and alcohol-soaked alleyways, in poor neighbourhoods, in defense of a lover's honour. Not the lover himself. In a beautiful house by a beach with a view of the water. Not a doctor.

Neal had told me that during the bad days of AIDS he'd lost dozens if not hundreds of patients. There was no cure, no life-prolonging combination of drugs, not even medicine for opportunistic infections. The early years they didn't even know all the types of illnesses that could hit nor what caused them. That's why he'd turned to research. He felt he had no choice. Someone had to figure out how to help properly.

I imagine caring. And giving of oneself. At the same time as turning off your feelings and emotions. Disassociating to survive.

Maybe the good signs were bad signs after all.

I don't know how many times he hit his partner during how many incidents and how long it lasted. I don't quite believe it happened and I do believe it happened. At least his partner might have had medical attention if he needed it.

Ross was right in telling me. Sometimes, to pull yourself away from something or somebody, you need a good reason.

I'll disassociate now. I'll place my physical attraction to Neal off in one corner. The warmth radiating from his skin, the strength in his torso, his eyes taking in light from my balcony. I'll place the intellectual attraction to him in another corner: his quirky collection of art deco vases; his taste in music: women jazz singers and sixties Motown; our shared favourite movies: *Strictly Ballroom* and European art-house films. I'll place the attraction to the idea of a relationship someplace else: imagining waking up in someone's arms, slow weekend mornings, forming new music with someone through the familiarity of voices. I'll tie my emotions in a knot and keep on walking.

I'm sad about me as much as about him. For years I thought that the ideal of perfect romance was a heterosexual plot out to get me. I railed against being told that I was incomplete without love. I proclaimed the value of friendship over fast-burning desire. But no matter how many times I think I've got it: peace of mind, a Nancy Sinatra swagger, self-containment like a ship in a bottle and how did it get there?, I return to an unreformed pre-feminist submissive pop song fantasy. I return to the heart, red like a traffic signal, strung up above the cars in this city, trying to trap the right motorist into stopping. This is a bad sign of something, I know.

Sometimes I pray. I remember as a child imitating the images that I saw on TV, kids from American sitcom families in the seventies, precocious child actors that would in real life grow up to have drug and alcohol addictions. I would kneel on the rug next to my bed and place my hands together tilted upwards. My parents, an atheist and an agnostic, would have been speechless at the sight. What did I pray for? I think it was just for the safety of my family, a request that's been granted so far.

I've never been religious though, apart from mild flirtations. Spiritual is what I'd call myself. But I'd have to admit: a prayer is a prayer, the two vowel sounds elided together, opening your mouth up to the world. Will your soul fly out or love come dashing in? And how will I know if it does? That it's not just some story I've spun, some complicated fantasy I've pieced together. That someone, be it god or guardian angel, a friend I haven't met yet, or a helpful stranger, will hear me calling.

Join my hands with someone else's. Show me a sign.